PUFFIN BOOKS

Fly Away Home

The eggs had moved. That's the first thing I noticed. Not only had they moved, but they were moving even then as I watched. I could hear this scratching sound and a pecking sound, like they were trying to break their way out! They were!

I stood, breathless, afraid to move, afraid to make a sound, my eyes fixed on the eggs.

The eggs jumped. And jumped. And wiggled. And then they began to crack.

All of them were doing it. It was like they all had the same idea at the exact same time—break out of the shells!

One after the other, the shells began rocking, breaking up. And then—I saw it—an eye! One big, wide eye looking at me.

"Oooh," I whispered. "Oh, just look at you."

Fly Away Home

**A novel by Patricia Hermes
from the screenplay by
Robert Rodat and Vince McKewin**

PUFFIN BOOKS

PUFFIN BOOKS

Published by the Penguin Group
Penguin Books Ltd, 27 Wrights Lane, London W8 5TZ, England
Penguin Books USA Inc., 375 Hudson Street, New York, New York 10014, USA
Penguin Books Australia Ltd, Ringwood, Victoria, Australia
Penguin Books Canada Ltd, 10 Alcorn Avenue, Toronto, Ontario, Canada M4V 3B2
Penguin Books (NZ) Ltd, 182–190 Wairau Road, Auckland 10, New Zealand

Penguin Books Ltd, Registered Offices: Harmondsworth, Middlesex, England

First published in the USA by Newmarket Press 1996
Published in Great Britain in Puffin Books 1997
1 3 5 7 9 10 8 6 4 2

Puffin Film and TV Tie-in edition first published 1997

Made and printed in England by Clays Ltd, St Ives plc

Fly Away Home:

The Novel

Chapter 1

Would I remember it? Dad said I would, but I didn't think so. Still, I couldn't help wondering as Dad turned the old pickup onto the road that led up the hill to . . . home. But it wasn't home. Not my real home, anyway. My real home was far away, in New Zealand. With Mum.

This was a different home. My dad's home. And I already hated it.

I peered through the window as we pulled up, looked at the house, the surrounding fields, the rain pouring down in torrents all around us.

No. I didn't remember it. Maybe because I had wanted to forget, maybe because it was so ugly. It was a pure, hateful, ugly, old-fashioned house with funny, crooked windows, in the middle of ugly, dripping fields with nothing around, probably nothing but wild creatures. Not like home. Not like my real home.

"It's just because it's raining," Dad said, like he was reading my mind. "There were two feet of snow here when I left." He pointed then. "Amy? Remember that? The swing set?"

I looked at this old, rusty set by the side of the house, the swings moving slowly back and forth in the rain.

Rain. Rain, just like the night it happened. Just like the night my mum died, that awful accident, with the truck bearing down on us. I remember seeing the truck coming, remember screaming, trying to scream, reaching for Mum. And the music, even after the crash and the ambulance sirens and the sounds of machines in the hospital where they took me—even then, inside my head, I could hear the music that was playing when it happened: "Fare thee well, my own true love." It haunted me, played over and over in my head. There is always music with Mum. Mine is my tuba, hers is . . . was . . . her singing.

"What's it been since you were last here, Amy?" Dad said, quietly. "Seven years?"

I kept staring out the window. "Nine," I said.

"Oh," Dad said. "That long."

Yes, that long. Nine years since Mum and Dad divorced. Nine years since Mum and I moved away and Mum got really big in her music career. I was really young then, and Dad has hardly ever come to see me since, but for a few times he came to us or we came here to Canada. Except now. Now that Mum was dead, I was stuck with him. And he with me. In this place that wasn't home.

I wrapped my arms tightly around myself as he pulled the truck up and stopped.

He looked out at the rain, then over at me. "Ready?" he said.

I wasn't. But we made a dash for the house anyway, ducking under dripping branches, hurrying for the shelter of the porch, and then into the kitchen.

Once inside, I stopped and looked around. Kitchen? This was a kitchen? This was a mess! There was a stove and a sink and some cabinets and all—but there was also stuff, stuff everywhere. Tools. A wing of a plane or a glider or something. A huge thing that looked like some sort of metal creature standing in the middle of the floor. Walls that were half up, half down, electrical wiring sticking out.

Right away, Dad started scooping stuff up—coffee cups, papers and mail, scraps of wood and tools.

"It'll be nice when it's finished," Dad said. "And see, over here. . . ." He pointed to a space on the counter top, pressed this button and a tiny, circular refrigerator popped up—out of the counter top! "See!" he said. "It's much more convenient than your standard fridge. You can see everything in it, and when you're done with it—bye, bye."

He pushed the button and it disappeared again. I just blinked at him.

"I won a design award for it," Dad said. "The Canadian Engineering Society Inventors award. And back there . . ." He pointed out the window and behind the house. "That's my workshop," he said. "You know about my inventions, right? You know. . . ."

"How long have you been doing this?" I asked, looking around the mess of the room.

"Remodeling?" Dad looked around the room, too, then as if seeing it for the first time. "Oh, for a while, actually, quite a while. I've been so busy in my workshop, I haven't had much spare time."

And no spare time to come see me, either.

"I mean," he went on quietly, "I haven't done any work on it in . . . I guess, nine years."

"Nine years?" I turned and stared at him.

He nodded. "Yes, uh, nine years. See, I stopped when you and your mom left. There didn't seem to be any . . . point."

I nodded. I understood that. There didn't seem to be any point in a lot of things lately.

"I'm very tired," I said.

"Oh," he said. "Your bedroom is upstairs. Remember?"

He turned, led the way to a staircase and we started up. Even the stairway was filled with junk.

"I didn't have a chance to fix your bedroom before I left," Dad said, turning and looking at me over his shoulder. "I mean, everything being so . . ."

He paused, then turned around again, and led the way down a small hall. He opened a door, reached in, switched on a light and we both stepped inside.

My room.

My room? This was my room?

It was even worse than the kitchen, more stuff here, piles of cartons, tools, scraps of metal, a welder's mask, goggles, even something that looked like an old airplane engine. And in one corner, a bed. A bed with a little teddy bear lying on the pillow.

"I, uh, ran out of storage space," Dad said from behind me. "You know, in the workshop and so. . . ."

He stopped.

For a long minute, neither of us said anything. I took a few steps further into the room. I was supposed to sleep here? Here in this mess?

How could he do this? How could he use my room this way? Didn't he know. . . .

I shook my head at myself. How could he know? How could he know that he'd have to fly to New Zealand, fly there and bring me home, and bury Mum and. . . .

"I'll get all the junk out of here tomorrow," Dad said quietly. "We'll make it just like you remember."

"I don't," I said.

"What?" he said, frowning at me.

"I don't remember it," I said. I picked my way across the floor, sat on the side of the bed. This whole place was such a mess. How could he live like this? How could I stand living here? How could I stand living—without Mum? I needed to be alone. And I wanted him out of here. Now.

I looked up at him. "I'm really tired," I said.

Dad nodded, and then for a long minute, he just looked at me. Then he looked around the room once more, then back at me. "Sure," he said quietly. "Goodnight."

He went out and closed the door.

When he was gone, I picked up the bear. Did I remember him? I concentrated, trying to remember the feel, testing to see if he felt familiar. Did I used to hold him? Did Mum put him in my arms and sing to me? Did I take the bear to bed, and did Mum . . .

I squeezed the bear hard for a long minute, then held him away and stared at him again. No, I didn't remember. I didn't remember the bear, and I·didn't remember this house, and I didn't remember this room. And I hardly remembered my father.

Suddenly, I heard voices downstairs, a . . . a woman's voice? And for this really dumb moment, I thought: Mum!

I jumped up, went to the door, opened it.

But, of course, it wasn't Mum. It wasn't even a woman talking at all. Just Dad, talking on the phone.

And even though I tried to imagine Mum there in the kitchen with him, I couldn't do it. Couldn't picture Mum here. In fact, I could hardly picture Mum's face at all anymore.

Chapter 2

My first thought when I woke up the next day was that I was back in the hospital. I could hear the sighing of that breathing machine, in and out and in and. . . .

I blinked, looked around me. I wasn't in the hospital. It was morning, and I was here, here in this place that wasn't home. And the sighing was the wind, blowing softly through the curtains. I turned over, looked out the window.

The sun was shining. That was something, anyway. No more rain.

I got up, went and looked out the window.

Outside, I could see a meadow covered in wild flowers, and some rolling fields and hills and, in the distance, a long slope of hillside. Down below the hill, I could just make out what looked like a marsh, with water and geese. Right out back, at the end of the drive, there was a big old barn, and through the open door I could see a tire swing.

I frowned, trying to recall something. Did I remember that? I felt like I remembered something, maybe Mum pushing me on that swing? But . . . no. Not really.

I sat for a long time at the window, looking out over it all. It was so lonely looking out there, just trees and meadows and hills, not a human being around, not even another house. No wonder Mum had left if it had always been so lonely here. The only thing moving were those geese, settled down below in the marsh.

And then I saw it . . . this . . . this thing! Something moving.

It was huge, moving crablike up the hill behind the house, creeping through the trees, out onto the hillside. It looked like a giant fly, or maybe a crab, but it was huge, as big as a small plane.

What was it?

A person, it looked like, a person with huge wings attached to its back.

But people don't have wings, not even here in Canada, I knew that.

I watched as the creature crept to the top of the hill, slowly, slowly. Then, at the top, it paused, seeming to catch its breath, and turned. And then, suddenly, it began running down the hill.

That's when I realized—Dad, my dad. It was my dad, with these wings attached, like a glider on his back, running, running down the hill—and then, just like that, he took off, was sailing through the air. And out of my sight.

I ran from my room, across the hall, to another window.

Yes. I could see him. There he was, sailing up, up, over the trees. Over the house. And was gone.

I raced down the stairs, almost tripping and killing myself over the stuff piled high there, ran outside to the porch.

Yes, I saw him, floating high over the hillside— flying, like some wild, winged creature. And then he turned, and began coming back. He was floating down, slowly, slowly, heading for the hillside. He was almost down, when a puff of wind caught him, and he suddenly jetted up again. Then the wind seemed to release him, and he came down. Hard. Crashed, and tumbled, over and over, and the wing part settled on top of him. And then, he wasn't moving at all.

Dead. He was dead. I just knew it.

He was a fool. And he was dead.

I started toward him, but just as I did, he suddenly threw off the wings, saw me looking, and grinned and waved at me. And then he yelled, this huge whooping sound, like, "Whoopee!" Like he was having fun!

Fun?. Almost killing yourself? Strange. He was a very strange man.

I turned, quickly, went back in the house.

I ran up the stairs, got dressed, and then waited. For some reason, I didn't want to see him. I still wanted to be alone, needed to be.

I waited till I heard him come in, waited till I heard him go through to his workshop. And then, when I was sure he was gone, I came downstairs and out. I had to get out of there, just out, somewhere.

Outside, I looked all around me. Where to go?

There was this huge hill in back, and I headed for that, made my way up there, to the place where my dad had just been flying—if you could call it flying. The grass was tall there, almost up to my waist, and here and there through the grasses, I saw birds flitting quickly, purposefully, as if on their way to something important. At the top of the hill, I could stand, looking out over the whole farm and the marsh below.

It was actually kind of pretty down below there, trees and wild flowers and a stone wall, and just beyond the wall, geese settled in to the marsh water, some of them seeming to be nesting, making families. There were a whole lot of geese, but just a few on nests, at least just a few that I could see.

For a long time, I stayed there watching them, wondering. What would it be like to be a wild bird? I wondered. What would it be like to sit on a nest, to hatch babies, to teach the babies things, how to swim and to fly? Would it be fun? Or just plain work? What would it be like to fly with them, to fly away, then back?

If I could fly away home to Mum . . . I looked up at the sky. Where was Mum? Was she in heaven, and was there really a heaven? Was it above us, like they used to tell us in Sunday school, high in the sky?

Silly, I told myself. I was being silly, like a little kid. I stood up, went down the hill, headed down to the marsh, stood at the edge of the water, looking at the geese.

They eyed me warily, one father goose strutting toward me, like he was warning me away.

"I won't bother you," I said softly, backing up a little. "I promise. I won't come near your babies."

He planted himself a few yards in front of me, his thick body shifting a bit side to side, the wind ruffling his feathers, his head slightly turned, one bright eye fixed on me.

I stayed there a while, but it was clear I was making him and the other geese nervous so, after a bit, I left. I went up the hill and around the house, heading for the barn. The tire swing I'd seen from my window hung right there in the open doorway.

I looked up at it, looked at the rope that was thrown over a rafter.

Would it still hold my weight? Did I used to swing on this?

I frowned, felt the rope, let it slide through my fingers. Yes, I remembered something—but what? Mum pushing me here, holding me in her lap?

I sighed, looked further around the barn.

There was stuff everywhere, just like in the house. A huge mirror, a trunk, piles of boxes and discarded bits of metal tubing and pipes, a dresser—all kinds of things.

For a while, I stared at the dresser. What was in it? My baby clothes? Mum's clothes?

I didn't go to look, though. Instead, I went further back into the barn, around a corner, and into a room . . . and almost screamed with fright. A spaceship! There was a space ship there, a REAL SPACE-SHIP.

What was it? I mean, what was it doing there?

Why would Dad have a spaceship in his barn?

Had he built this, too? One of his inventions?

I started back to the house, then changed my mind and went around the side to his workshop. I could hear him in there, hear the sound of this machine going, hear sparks shooting out.

I stepped inside.

Dad was up on a high scaffold, wearing a mask, and he was welding something to this enormous monster thing, this thing that looked like a huge dragon.

When he saw me in the doorway, he stopped the machine, pulled off his mask.

"Hey!" he said. "I saw you this morning. You didn't know I could fly, did you? What did you think?"

I just shrugged. "About you breaking your neck, you mean?" I said.

He made a face. "Actually," he said, "for me that was a pretty decent landing."

I turned away. "Then I'd give it up," I said.

He didn't answer.

"I saw a spaceship in the barn," I said.

"Yeah!" he said. "You remember that, right? That's our lunar lander. I was building it the winter your mom . . . left. I guess she thought I was crazy. I mean, I had no money. I had a dislocated shoulder at the time. It was freezing cold and. . . ."

"Why?" I said, turning back to him. "Why did you build it?"

"Why?" Dad frowned down at me. "Because. I loved it. Loved the whole moon trip. I mean, everybody has forgotten how exciting it was. Jeez, the moon, Amy! Another world."

He sounded so excited. So . . . weird.

"It's a perfect replica," Dad said, 'as if that explained it. "It's an exact and perfect replica."

"Right," I said. "Every home should have one."

"Well," he said. "I've been offered a lot of money for it."

I pointed at the dragon or whatever it was. "What's that?" I said.

"He's going to a museum in Montreal," Dad said. "I'm just finishing him." Dad tilted his head, looked at the dragon. "Does he need a goatee? Or should he be clean shaven?"

"Give him a beard," I said. "Then he'll look like you. Only not as crazy."

For a minute, he didn't answer. And then he said, very slowly, quietly, "Listen. I'm really behind on my

17

work, late delivering him. So I'm going to be trying to get caught up."

I shrugged.

"I mean," he continued, "I'll probably be here in the shop a lot, okay?"

I just looked at him. "You don't have to hold my hand," I said. "I'm not a baby."

And I turned and left.

Chapter 3

It was morning and I was up super early, long before Dad was up, long before it was time for the school bus. I stood at the back door looking out over the hill, looking down toward the marsh, thinking. Thinking about how NOT to go to school.

I'd gone for two days now, and I wasn't going back—people making fun of my accent, staring at my clothes. Like they were best dressed in the whole world, right, with their stupid baggy pants and rings in their ears—and in their noses! I was not going back. But I had to figure out how to avoid it.

I just stood there, thinking, eating my cereal, looking out. Plotting. Maybe I could sneak down to the barn, hide in the grasses till the bus was gone. I wasn't sure just what to do, but I knew I'd figure it out.

I had to figure out other stuff, too. Like about Susan, my dad's friend, who had come over last night. She got there just when Dad and I were getting ready for dinner. Dad had made this disgusting stuff—a stew, with chili and beef and spices—and peanut butter! I wouldn't eat it.

Susan had seemed all embarrassed and awkward when she spoke to me, like I was a visitor from Mars or something. Well, I lived here now, and she was stuck with having me here, whether she liked it or not. And clearly it was NOT, anyone could see that, even though she tried hard not to show it.

Right away, there was something about her I didn't like, maybe because she tried too hard to be sweet. Sickly sweet, Mum would have said.

She and Dad had this mushy reunion, her falling all over him, hugging his neck, rubbing his back.

Gross.

Then later, when I had gone upstairs to bed, I had eavesdropped. I heard her tell Dad that I was different than she had expected, more "complicated." I didn't know what she meant by that exactly, but I knew it was better than being fake sweet like her. And what did she mean, different than she'd expected? What had she "expected" anyway? What business of hers was it to expect anything?

I know Dad wanted her to stay—maybe she was used to staying, I didn't know. But she said no, said she wasn't even sure she should be there, not with me here.

Well, that was one thing she was right about.

I put down my cereal bowl, stared again out the window. What to do? Another day to face—another lonely day. Another stupid day at school. I wasn't going. No matter how many times Dad pushed me out the door to that school bus, I wouldn't go.

There was a noise outside then, a loud, roaring kind of engine sound. The school bus already?

I frowned, looked at my watch. No, much too early.

The sound came again. Louder. Then I heard another sound, geese honking, calling, and then the engine again, revving up.

I bent closer to the window, peered out.

What was it? Where was it?

20

Way down, down by the marsh, I could just see something—something big, something yellow. A bull-dozer? Yes, a bulldozer moving, with a roaring, crunching sound. It was moving surprisingly quickly for something so big, and as it roared forward trees collapsed in its path, falling to earth, one on top of another.

I could see the earth swelling up, rising in big waves of brown and green as the machine plowed forward, trees and marsh and everything tumbling in its path. And the geese, they were frantic, squawk-ing, honking, calling.

The sound was awful, scary almost, as things crunched and the geese honked. Then . . . some-thing else happened.

Dad. He came flying past me, out of his bedroom and down the stairs, wearing nothing but his under-wear.

He practically shoved me aside, tore open the door, and went flying down the hillside, waving his arms madly.

"Stop! Stop!" I heard him yelling. "This is against the law. We haven't voted yet. You son . . ."

He was jumping up and down in the grass, yelling, waving his arms, leaping around like some wildman or like some freakish cartoon creature.

I saw him bend then, pick up a rock. Then he hurled it at the bulldozer. Picked up another. Threw it. And another. And another.

He was crazy. He had gone absolutely crazy, flinging rock after rock, yelling and swearing, jump-ing up and down.

He was absolutely crazy. No wonder Mum had left him.

I backed up, turned, ran up the stairs to my room. I pulled off my nightgown, threw on some underwear and a shirt, grabbed my overalls, pulled them on. I was getting out of here. Out of here, away from this crazy. But where? Not to school.

Suddenly, I realized the sound outside had stopped, the roaring, crunching sound, although I could still hear the racket from the geese.

Why had the bulldozer stopped? Had Dad hit the driver with a rock? Killed him?

I stayed absolutely still for a moment, listening. Nothing. It was just very quiet, inside and out.

"Amy?"

I turned. It was Dad, wearing a robe now, standing in my doorway.

"Amy," he said. "Sorry about that."

I just shrugged, went on dressing. Out of here. I was getting out of here. He was just too weird.

"Amy," Dad said. "See, these people are trying to build right next to our place here. A golf course. A hotel, a mall thing. We've been fighting it, see? But today they came and started on it. Without even a vote. We're planning a vote, but they came anyway. I made him stop for now, but. . . ."

"I don't care," I said. I finished buttoning my straps, then bent to pull on my shoes.

"But let me explain," Dad said. "I know I looked a bit. . . ."

I spun around. "I don't care!" I said. "See? I don't care about it, not any of it."

He was just looking at me.

"And I'm not going to school anymore," I said. "I'd rather die!"

He opened his mouth, closed it.

And you're weird! This whole place is weird. I hate it. I hate you! I want Mum back. Even though the words began welling up inside me, I didn't say them, couldn't say them, because suddenly, tears were choking me. I just collapsed on my bed, face down, and began to cry.

"Amy?" Dad said. He came over, stood beside the bed.

I buried my face in the bear, pressed his prickly fur against my cheek.

"Why did all this happen?" I said.

No answer. But I could tell Dad was still there, could hear his breath, catching a little.

"Why can't I wake up and have everything like it was?" I asked.

He still didn't answer.

The tears were coming harder now, the first time since in the hospital when I heard Mum died. The pain was there again, the pain in my chest. It is a pain, where she's gone from me, a real pain, like in your heart. That's what people mean when they say your heart is breaking. It really feels like that. It does.

"Amy," Dad said.

"Tell me that," I said. I turned, looked up at him. I wanted to sit up and . . . and do something. Hit him, hurt him.

Why did it have to be like this?

It wasn't his fault, I knew that. He couldn't help it if Mum was gone. Dead.

But why couldn't he be like her—at least a little bit? Why couldn't he understand? She would have.

Dad put out one hand to me then. He opened his mouth, like he was going to say something. But then he just closed it. He didn't say a word. He just kept standing there, one hand out, shaking his head.

I turned away, buried my head in my bear.

Then, after a long minute, I heard him leave. I heard him go out, heard the door close quietly behind him.

Like he didn't understand. Like he didn't even care.

Chapter 4

I did go to school that day. Dad practically shoved me out the door, threw my jacket and my books and my lunch money at me, made me get on the bus. Not that it mattered that much. It might have been even worse, staying home, watching for one more weird thing he'd do. I didn't speak to anyone that whole day, though, not on the bus to school, not in school, not on the bus coming home, not one single person. I just pretended they didn't exist, just like they pretended I didn't exist, and when the bus dropped me off, I didn't go into the house to see my dad, either.

Instead, I walked around back toward the marsh. The bulldozer was gone, but its mess was everywhere. Trees were uprooted, earth overturned, branches and grasses smashed and lying every which way on the ground.

The marsh was wrecked, too, mud everywhere, the reeds and grasses all torn up. And the geese were gone. I stood quietly, looking all around, but I didn't see a single goose anywhere.

The whole place was so sad looking, so forlorn. How could one bulldozer do all this damage? And why? Dad had said they weren't supposed to do this. Yet they had. They'd made a mess, a big, sad mess, and they shouldn't have. Maybe for once Dad hadn't been totally crazy.

25

Carefully, I stepped over some heaped dirt and piles of branches, went out further into the marsh.

I stood silently, looking all around, listening, hoping. But no sounds. No geese. Not even a single bird calling nor a frog croaking—nothing, like all life had been chased away.

I went further into the marsh then, my feet squishing in the water and mud.

Then—I don't really think I was looking for anything—but maybe I was. Suddenly, I saw something—eggs—a nest of them. Six eggs lying together in a nest, six perfect eggs. And a seventh, lying crushed and smashed. But no mama goose.

I looked around again.

No papa goose, either. No mama. No papa. Just the eggs.

Had the parents been killed? Or just scared away? I stood very still, peering into the marsh grasses, into the brush. Perhaps, if I didn't move, maybe the parent geese would show themselves. Maybe they'd just been scared away, but would come back.

I stood perfectly still for a long time, a very long time. But nothing. I didn't see a single goose, not even far out in the marsh, and I didn't hear one, either. Surely, if they were still here, I'd hear their rustling, honking.

But I heard nothing.

I looked back at the eggs. What would happen to them? I wondered. How could they hatch? How could they live without a mother to warm them, a father to protect them?

For a long time, I stood there, thinking. If I found a warm place for them, if I kept them warm . . .

I shook my head. No. That wasn't possible. I

mean, nobody could take the place of a mama goose.

But why not? I asked myself. If they were kept warm, they might hatch even without a mama goose.

I shook my head again. Not possible.

Then I thought of my mum. Strange, I not only thought of her, I heard her in my head as clear as if she were really talking to me. Why not? I heard her say. Who says it's not possible, Amy? Besides, I think you'd be a really good mum.

I smiled then, looked down at the eggs, lying there naked, unprotected, cold. Could I care for them? Of course, I couldn't care for them here. But maybe I could find—or make—a place for them somewhere. Where, though? My room? No. Dad would have a fit over that once they hatched. Maybe in the barn? Yes, the barn would probably be best.

I looked down at the eggs once more. "I'll be right back," I whispered to them. Then I took off running, heading for the barn.

When I got there, I slowed, thinking. Should I ask Dad to help? No. He'd say no, he'd say I had to pay attention to school, to. . . .

Better not to say anything at all.

In the barn, I looked around, searching for the perfect place. It would have to be a quiet place. A warm place. And most of all, a safe place. No owls or rats could get to them.

I stood for a long while, thinking, then focused on the dresser. Slowly, I went over to it, opened up a drawer. Yes, in the drawer it would be safe. And warm. No owls or rats could get in there if I closed it tightly.

But then I wondered: What happens to a baby goose that gets hatched in a drawer—without a mother?

Well, better than not getting hatched at all, right?

I looked through the stuff in the drawer. It was mostly baby clothes, old stuff, kind of mildewy by now. My things? From when I was a baby? And there were dresses and scarfs and some hats—Mum's things?

Then I found something—the best something—a snuggly, that thing that mothers use to carry babies in. It's like a big, soft bag, and you put it against your chest, put the straps over your shoulders, and then put the baby in it. It holds the baby close to you.

I lifted out the snuggly, looked at it. It must have been mine, the one Mum used to carry me in. For a minute, I pressed it against my face, breathing in deeply. But I couldn't smell Mum, couldn't feel her there, either.

It would work if I was careful. I could use it for the eggs, to carry them here! I tucked it under my arm, raced for the marsh again.

Down at the marsh, I tiptoed through the water, found the nest hidden in the reeds. The eggs were still there, all safe. But for the one.

I slid the straps of the snuggly over my shoulders and fastened the other straps around me. Then, very gently, I began lifting out the eggs, one at a time. They were smooth to the touch, but cold. Had the babies inside died already?

No, they'd be okay. I'd warm them up. "It's okay," I whispered to them. "You're cold now, but you'll warm up. You'll be okay."

After I had them all scooped up, I had another thought. Maybe there were other nests, other motherless babies.

Carefully, then, I picked my way through the marsh, my feet squishing in the water, looking. And I found it—them! Two more nests. Ten more motherless eggs.

At each nest, I stopped, then gently, carefully picked up the eggs. "You'll be all right," I told each one as I picked it up. "You will. I promise." And I held it against my face a moment, then lowered it into the snuggly, being careful not to let them hit against one another.

Sixteen eggs. Sixteen motherless babies.

Afterward, when I had scoured the marsh, when I was certain there were no more eggs, I carefully carried my sixteen eggs up to the barn.

In the barn, I put the snuggly down very carefully, then went to work. First, I opened the top dresser drawer and lined it with things I found—an old shawl, baby clothes, some soft diapers, Mum's hat. I shaped and patted it, making the softest, nicest nest I could make. A lovely nest. Then, when it was ready, I began very gently taking the eggs out of the snuggly. I laid each one, one at a time, in the new nest, all sixteen of them. Perfect.

When I was finished, I stood back and looked. Now what? It would be warm in there, especially with the drawer closed. But would it be warm enough?

Then I remembered something. In school, one Easter time, we hatched baby chicks. We did it with lights, putting a light in the box where we kept the eggs. We made our own hatching box.

I knew just what to use.

But how to get it? If Dad wasn't looking, if he was absorbed in his welding . . .

I closed the dresser drawer, ran from the barn to the workshop, and stopped outside, listening. I could hear Dad working, hear his welding equipment going. Quietly, I slid open the door, looked around. Dad was up on the scaffolding, wearing a welder's mask, working with his torch. There was a lot of noise and sparks shooting out, and he didn't see me or, at least, he didn't act as if he saw me. He kept on working, intent on his project. I saw exactly what I needed. It was on the floor right in front of me: his worklight, this huge lightbulb inside a wire cage, with a long electrical cord attached, along with an extension cord. Perfect.

I crouched down, reached for it, picked it up, looked up at Dad.

He still hadn't seen me, was still bent over, adjusting something under the dragon's chin. I backed out, holding the light, pulling the cord along with it. Once I was outside, I very quietly closed the door behind me, then raced back for the barn, clutching the light.

In the barn, I found an outlet, plugged the light in, turned it on. Then I slid open the drawer again. The eggs lay there, side by side, nestled in their blankets and soft old diapers.

Carefully, I slid the light into the drawer, put my hand over the lighbulb. Yes! Warm. It got very warm. The babies would love it, would think their mum had come back.

I smiled, breathed deeply. Then, I settled the light in there, making sure it didn't touch any of the eggs.

When I was sure everything was just right, no eggs touching any other eggs, the light not too hot or anything, I carefully slid the drawer closed.

I stood back and looked at it, at the small line of light shining out of the drawer. Yes, it was fine. Warm. Safe.

I put my mouth close to the drawer. "You'll be all right, now," I whispered to them. "I promise. Even without your mum, you're going to be just fine."

Chapter 5

Next day, I was frantic to check on my eggs. I'd been thinking of them all day in school and all through supper, too. It had been an entire day since I had put them in their nest drawer, and I was worried. Were they warm enough? Were they too warm? Were they hatched yet? I had tried to check on them early that morning, but couldn't, because everything turned suddenly crazy. I mean, crazy.

I had gone downstairs early, tiptoeing down, my shoes and jacket and books under my arm, knowing I had to be quiet not to wake Dad.

Silently, I dropped my things on the couch, tiptoed for the back door.

That's when I heard it. This yowl from behind me.

I spun around, stared. This figure—this person, this man—was rising up from the bundle of quilts and stuff on the couch, from where I had just dumped my shoes and school books.

"Stop them! Stop them!" he was yelling.

"What?" I yelled back. "What? Who are you?"

He rubbed a hand over his face. "Oh," he said, "it was terrible. They were coming at me through the frozen food section. It was just terrible. Their lips were so blue."

I backed up toward the door.

He shook his head, blinked at me.

32

"Ooh," he said. He rubbed his hands over his face. "Oh. I'm David. You've got to be Amy. I gave you silly putty one Christmas. You ate it. You'd eat anything that wasn't nailed down."

I just kept staring at him.

"Right, Tom?" he said. "Didn't she?"

I turned around. Dad had appeared in the doorway behind me, wrapped in his bathrobe, his hair all rumpled up.

"Remember, Tom?" this person said. "She took a bite out of a slipper once, I remember. Didn't she?"

I turned to Dad. "Who is he?" I said. "What's he doing here?"

"He's your uncle," Dad said. "He's David. He came to help me catch up with my work."

"Right," David said. "Thomas makes me come here and be his beast of burden. I lug pig iron for Michelangelo here."

That's when the bus honked, and Dad practically threw me out the door, yelling that I had to go to school, that's where you belong, every day, blah, blah, blah. Even though I kept shouting, "Wait!" he practically shoved me out the door. So I went. To the longest day ever. Now it was late afternoon, supper time, and I was home, and now there was another big delay. David. Again.

Dad and Susan had gone to a meeting about the marsh, leaving me with this David person. But first, they had given directions about how to heat up dinner and what time I went to bed, like I needed a baby-sitter or something.

Finally, though, they were gone, and David and I were settled down to dinner. All I could think about was how to sneak out to the barn.

"Uh, David," I said, putting down my fork and pushing myself away from the table. "I'm finished. I have to. . . ."

"I really don't understand my brother," David interrupted me, like he didn't even hear me speaking. "Susan's good looking and she can cook. Did you know she made this stuff?" He held up his forkful of stew.

I nodded. Susan could cook, I'd say that for her. Better than Dad, anyway.

"She's good looking and she can cook," David went on. "Marry her, I say!"

"Is he going to marry her?" I said, alarmed. I didn't want that! I mean, Dad by himself was enough. With super-sweet Susan . . .

"Nah," David said. "He's scared to. Hey, she's the first girlfriend he's had in years. It used to be such a drag coming here. Nothing worse than when you mooch off your brother and there aren't any women around."

He wasn't looking at me as he talked, just bent over his plate, wolfing down his food like he hadn't eaten in a month.

I looked over at the back door, at the flashlight on the chair there.

"Uh, David," I said. "I have homework to do and. . . ."

"Is there more?" David said, holding out his plate.

I just rolled my eyes, then snatched the plate from him and went to the stove. I ladled out a big thing of stew for him, brought it back.

"Thanks," he said. "And she makes good money, too, Susan does. "She's a farrier. Know what that is?"

I didn't, and I didn't care. "Listen," I said again. "I

have homework to do. And then, maybe I'll take a walk or something."

"It means she shoes horses," David went on, his head bent over his plate, stuffing in his food, talking with his mouth full. Mum would have murdered him for eating like that. "But not just any old horse," he went on. "She's got a concession out at the track. Class hooves. We're talking some very healthy bucks here."

I got up, went to the sink. "I'll do the dishes," I said.

"Hey," David said. "Maybe I should go for a dying skill, too. You know, I got two degrees that didn't work. I have one in aerospace engineering and a BA in literature. Forget about it. No, your dad did it right. He followed his heart. He's always done that. From art, to inventions, to flying. Did he ever tell you how he started flying?"

I went back to the table, snatched his plate right out from in front of him. He was almost finished anyway. Or he should be.

"Because of Odd Job," David said. "That's why."

"Excuse me?" I said.

"Odd Job," David said. "That was the name of an old goose used to be on our uncle's farm."

I turned around. "Dad liked geese?" I said.

David shrugged. "Don't know, but he liked Odd Job. Odd Job was hysterical. He'd had his wings clipped and couldn't fly, but he didn't seem to know that. He used to run down this big hill behind the barn. Like a 747 on takeoff. He'd run and run and run, and somehow, just clear the fence and get airborne. And then crash and burn in the pond. And then he'd shake himself and take off again."

David got up, went over and plopped himself in front of the TV. "Funny, isn't it?" he said. "Thomas flies because of Odd Job. Who would have thought?"

He turned on the TV to a wrestling match, settled back in his chair, smiling. Wrestling! The dumbest, most boring sport anyone has ever watched.

At least if he stayed absorbed in the wrestling . . .

But he didn't—stay absorbed, that is. Which was just fine with me. Because in about two minutes, I could see he was falling asleep. I could see his head nodding, then snapping back up, then nodding again.

Probably because he had stuffed himself. Or because wrestling was boring for him, too.

Whatever. But goody for me, because now I was free!

I headed for the back door, picked up the flashlight.

I took one last look at David nodding in the chair, waited another minute till I was sure he'd gone bye-bye, then slipped outside and raced for the barn.

Free! Free! To see my eggs.

In the barn, I lay the flashlight on the floor next to the dresser, then slowly, carefully, slid open the drawer.

The eggs had moved. That's the first thing I noticed. Not only had they moved, but they were moving even then as I watched. I could hear this scratching sound and a pecking sound, like they were trying to break their way out! They were!

I stood, breathless, afraid to move, afraid to make a sound, my eyes fixed on the eggs.

The eggs jumped. And jumped. And wiggled. And then they began to crack.

All of them were doing it. It was like they all had

the same idea at the exact same time—break out of the shells!

One after the other, the shells began rocking, breaking up. And then—I saw it—an eye! One big, wide eye looking at me.

"Oooh," I whispered. "Oh, just look at you."

I reached in, slowly, carefully. I touched one, just one finger on its little head. "Look at you," I whispered.

He began clucking—or peeping—or whatever it is he was doing, making little soft sounds.

Then another egg cracked and another eye appeared, another gosling. The eggs continued to jump, move, crack. It took a long while, a very long while. The whole time I stood there, staring, hardly daring to breathe. They had done it! They had hatched. My eggs. My goslings.

Soon, all of them had done it, had cracked open their eggs and were wobbling around, their necks seeming too weak to hold up their heads. But they were out. Out of the shells and watching me, their bright eyes fixed on me.

I kept my hand in the drawer, not to pick them up, not yet. They were too wet, too slippery. Too little. I just wanted to touch them, to put one finger on each head, to welcome each one.

"You are beautiful," I whispered. "Every single one of you. You are simply beautiful."

I don't know how long I stood there looking at them. A long time. A long, long time. Once, I thought about David and whether he had awakened, but just once. I figured he was probably still asleep or, if he did wake up, he'd probably figure I was asleep upstairs.

Then suddenly, I don't know why, but I knew I couldn't leave them there. I just couldn't. Not yet, anyway. They couldn't spend their first hours in the world out here alone.

I bent over, pushed around some of the straw that was on the floor, made a huge bed out of it; built it up around the sides, like an enormous nest. Then, very gently, carefully, I lifted each gosling out of the drawer and set it in the nest on the floor. I made the sides even higher, so they couldn't get out and away.

By then, it was late, very late, I knew. I was really tired, as tired as if I had done all the work hatching, not them. So I lay down in the straw nest with them, stretched out, just watching them while they crept and scrabbled all over me, their tiny feet feeling like tiny, spidery bugs as they climbed over my arms and legs and even my face.

I put my arm up behind me, pillowing my head, smiling at the goslings. Names. I'd have to come up with names. Sixteen names for sixteen babies.

I thought of names from books I had read, people I'd known. Frederica. That was a good name. But I wondered how you could tell which one needed a boy's name and which a girl.

Long John. That was a good one; I remembered that from a book. And Ralph. Yes. Ralph, the goose.

I smiled at one gosling, who had crept right up against my shoulder and was already snuggling in to me. "Muffy," I whispered. "That's a good name for you."

They seemed to like hearing my voice, because they all began huddling closer to me then, some nestled in at my shoulders, some around my knees.

"That's right, guys," I whispered to them. "You snuggle in here."

That's the last thing I remember until I heard Dad calling, frantically, and I awoke to a light shining in my face.

"Amy!" He was bent over me, looking terrified. "Amy!" he said. "My god, Amy, I thought I'd lost you." He bent and hugged me, took off his coat, laid it over me. "You must be freezing," he said.

I looked around, frowning. Where was I? Suddenly I remembered.

I tugged at the coat, tried to cover the goslings. But it was no use. Dad had seen them. Now he was looking right at me, this puzzled look on his face.

"They . . . hatched," I said.

Dad was quiet for a minute. Then he nodded. "Yes. I see."

"Can I . . . can I keep them?" I whispered.

For a long minute, he just looked at me. Then he put a hand on my head. "I don't see why not," he said, smiling. "I don't see why not."

Chapter 6

By next day, I had brought the whole lot of them into the house, into the kitchen with me. David's the one who told me about how they had to be fed—every two hours, he said.

I set them all down on the kitchen table, gave them some cereal, the same cereal I was eating. They loved it! Loved everything about it. They ate it, and walked in it—and they also pooped in it.

Oh, well, they were babies.

But I couldn't go to school, not if they had to be fed every two hours.

I settled down at the table with them, smiling. They were all over the place, like little kittens or something.

"Oh, my god!"

I whirled around.

It was Dad—standing at the kitchen door, sleepy looking—and panicky looking, too. "What a mess!" he said.

"I'm feeding them," I said. "Every two hours. David told me."

"Every two hours?" Dad said.

I nodded. "They need a lot of attention, too."

Dad came further into the room, frowning, scrunching up his nose. "They need to learn where to poop," he said.

40

I shrugged. "They're just babies. What do you expect?"

Dad sat down, lifted a gosling out of the bowl in front of him, put him on the floor. "They can't stay in the house," he said.

I glared at him. "They do. They have to!" I said. "They're too young. Owls and cats and stuff will get them. They'll die if you put them outside."

"Amy," Dad said.

"No!" I said. "I mean it. You said I could keep them."

Dad took a deep breath. "Okay, okay. But . . ."

There was a sound outside—a bus honking, the school bus.

"That's your bus!" Dad said.

"I'm not going," I said.

"Amy!" Dad said.

"Then you have to promise me you'll feed them," I said.

"I'll feed them!" Dad said.

"Every two hours," I said. "And you have to promise you won't put them outside."

"Amy!" Dad said.

"Promise!" I said.

"Okay, okay, I promise," Dad said. "I promise, I promise, I promise."

The bus was honking again.

I looked down at my goslings, scattered all over the place, on the floor, the table, even a few of them had settled themselves like people on the chairs. "I'll be back guys, don't worry," I told them. I looked at Dad then. "Are you sure you can handle this?" I said.

He pointed to the door. "Go!"

I went. But I worried all day.

I shouldn't have worried, though. When I got back, they were all fine. One thing I'm learning about Dad is that if he promises something, he means it. When I got home that day, he'd done lots of good stuff for my geese.

First, he had cared for them all day. He had also gone to the Animal Regulation Office where he met this guy Glen who is an animal protection officer. He told Glen about the goslings, and he promised to come out soon to teach me about how to raise them.

After that, each day, Dad and David cared for them during the day, and then after school I played with them. It was so cool. They were only a few days old, but already they could walk and even run. But the best was that they followed me. No matter what I did or where I went—sixteen litle goslings went with me. They lined up in a regular line, like little kids in school and, when I ran and clucked to them or made little sounds at them, they followed me. They followed me everywhere, up and over stone walls, through the grass, everywhere.

I didn't make them run far though, or anything. They were still really little, and they got tired easily. The littlest one limped—I needed to watch out for him especially.

I could tell Susan was liking them, and David was, too. I wasn't so sure about Dad, though. He seemed a little grumpy about it—maybe because they made such a mess in the house.

One afternoon, after we had had a little exercise, David and I took them to the barn for a while.

Susan was going to stay and make supper—which

was fine with me. Dad's cooking was beginning to get to me.

"So have you named them all?" David asked.

I nodded. "Mostly all. That's Frederica," I said, pointing. "And that's Long John and Stinky—that's because he likes to play in the mud. And there's Ralph and Muffy. I'm still working on the others."

David reached down and very gently picked up the littlest one, the one that limped. "What's his name?" he said.

"I haven't named him yet," I said.

"Why does he limp?" David asked.

I shrugged. "Don't know. He was born like that. I was thinking of Gimpy."

David nodded, then set the gosling down very gently. "Yeah, but he might get a complex," he said. "Like that's his identity or something."

"Oh," I said. "Yeah. I didn't think of that."

"How about Igor?" David said.

"Igor?"

"You know, Dr. Frankenstein's Igor?"

David got up, limped around, his hands drawn up like claws in front of him, his face twisted up, his head on one side—his impression of a limping monster.

I had to laugh. "Sounds good to me. Igor it is. Let's go in to supper."

I stood up. "Come on, gooses," I said. I made this clucking sound, then added a little "Hey, hey, hey," and they all ran right after me, out of the barn and into the house.

While we ate, the goslings ran all over the place. Susan kept picking them up, rescuing them from getting stepped on, but she was smiling the whole time. I could tell she definitely was beginning to like them.

After supper, when Glen got there, Susan made a great big bowl of popcorn, and I sat in the living room eating it, sharing it with the goslings. I was happy to sit and just collapse in front of the TV. Being a mother goose was turning out to be a big job.

Dad and Susan and Glen sat behind me in the kitchen, talking, but I could hear every word they said.

"It's amazing how they follow her, isn't it?" Dad said. "Did you see before?"

"It's called imprinting," Glen answered. "The first living thing the geese see when they're born they think is their mother. They'll follow her everywhere."

So they did think I was their mother!

"Amazing," Susan said.

"Well, they're creatures of instinct," Glen answered. "But all in all, pretty dumb."

I looked over at him. Dumb?

"So how big should the cages be?" Dad asked.

"Cages?" Glen answered. "What cages?"

"You know," Dad said. "For the geese. For when they get bigger."

Glen threw back his head and laughed. "No, no, you don't need cages. It's a lot easier than that."

"I don't follow," Dad said.

Glen laughed again, tucking his sunglasses into his pocket. Then he took out a pair of nail clippers, and began clipping his fingernails—right there at the table! Talk about dumb!

He looked up and smiled at Dad. "Okay," he said. "First of all, you've got to understand that geese are very tough animals. Like rats."

Susan caught my eye, and she raised her eyebrows. I just shrugged. We both looked again at Glen.

"Right. Rats," Glen said. "I mean, the way the geese have been displaced over the years, you would think they'd be extinct by now. But they've learned to adapt. Learned to find places to go."

"Like where?" Dad said. "Where do they go?"

Glen nodded. "That's the problem," he said. "I get complaints all the time about them on golf courses or people's lawns. Ultimately, that's why the law was created."

"What law?" Dad said.

"Domestically raised geese have to be rendered flightless," Glen answered. "It's Ontario Act 093-14."

Glen got up from the table, then came into the living room where I was.

I reached out both arms, scooped my goslings closer to me.

"It's better known as pinioning," Glen said. "It's really a simple procedure."

He reached down and snatched up one of my goslings.

"No!" I said. "Put him down, please! They're my geese."

Glen smiled down at me. "It's Amy, isn't it?"

I nodded, but I kept my hand out for my gosling.

"The fact is, Amy," Glen said, "these geese belong to the Crown."

I looked over at Dad and Susan. They were whispering together, as worried looking as I felt.

I turned back to Glen. "Crown? Crown who?" I said.

Glen just laughed. "The Queen of England, that's

who," he said. "And she made a law that we all have to follow. For the good of the people."

He was still holding my gosling—Muffy, it was. He had her in one hand, and the nail clippers in the other.

"It's really a simple procedure." He looked down at me. "And really quite painless."

He raised the nail clippers, stretched out Muffy's wing and. . . .

I jumped up. "What are you doing!" I yelled.

"Believe me, Amy," Glen said. "The bird doesn't feel a thing."

"Let go of her!" I yelled.

"Stop that, Glen!" Dad yelled. "Wait!"

Glen put the tip of Muffy's wing right inside the mouth of the nail clippers. That's when I hit him. I grabbed the popcorn bowl and hit him with it, bopped him hard right over the head. But he didn't let go of Muffy. For just a minute, he just stood there, shaking his head, and then he bent to the clippers again.

By then, Dad had come charging into the room and had grabbed Glen around the waist, tying him up like a bear.

I snatched Muffy from his hands, scooped her and my other goslings into the popcorn bowl, and escaped with all of them to the bathroom—where I locked myself in. Locked them in, too. Safe. We were all safe. My heart was pounding like crazy, but we were safe. I leaned back against the door. Through the door, I could hear the fight going on.

"What do you think you're doing!" Dad was yelling.

"I'm trying to help!" Glen yelled back. "What do

you think is going to happen when those birds fly? They'll try to migrate in a few weeks and be dead a month later."

I bent over them, put my hands around them, hoping they didn't hear. "No you won't!" I whispered to them. "Don't listen to him."

"I can't believe you were going to do that!" Dad yelled back.

"You listen closely," Glen said. "Those birds could carry parasites and disease. And they could pass it on to wild flocks. And that, my friend, is not going to happen on my watch. They're getitng clipped, one way or the other."

"Don't let me see you on my place again," Dad said. "Get! Out!"

"If those birds fly," Glen said, "I'll confiscate them."

"Stay off my property!" Dad yelled.

I heard the door slam.

Gone. He was gone. But he'd come back. I knew he would.

And no way would I let him get my goslings. No way. If I had to stay in the bathroom with them forever.

Chapter 7

All night I stayed in the bathroom. I made a bed with towels for myself in the tub and put some water in the sink for my goslings. I knew that Glen person would come back, and he might sneak in here in the dark, right into the house. But he couldn't get into the bathroom. The door was locked, and the window was too small for anyone to climb in.

Too bad if Dad or Susan needed the bathroom. There was another one upstairs.

They were really upset. Dad sounded kind of mad at me. He kept talking to me through the door, promising me that he wouldn't let anybody hurt my goslings, that he hadn't known Glen was going to do that.

Maybe. But he should have known! And Glen! How could they call him an animal protection person? He wasn't protecting them. He was hurting them. Making them so they couldn't fly!

Anyway, Dad was awfully upset. I heard him tell Susan that he wasn't any better a father now than he was when I was younger. I heard him threatening to take the door off the hinges. If he did that, I'd run away so far he'd never find me. And I'd take my goslings with me.

I also heard something else—something that made

me kind of sad for Susan, maybe even helped me understand her a little.

She and Dad had finally given up trying to make me come out of the bathroom, and they went outside. They were sitting on the back steps talking, but it was just outside the bathroom window, so I could hear every word they said. That's when Dad said that thing about not being a good father, and Susan said, well, at least you're here. She told Dad that she'd never known her father, that he left when she was just a little baby. That's the part that made me sad. It must be sad not to know your own father.

But I couldn't help wondering if her father was as weird as mine. That's the last thing I remember before falling asleep. Next thing I knew, it was early morning, and I could hear voices outside in the kitchen—Dad and some man. Not David. Someone else, someone talking about flying and stuff.

I looked all around me. Some of my goslings were in the tub with me and some in the sink. I counted them—thirteen, fourteen, fifteen . . . one was missing. Igor. Where was Igor?

I stood up, looked around.

"Igor!" I said. Then I saw him. I snatched him up—out of the toilet, where he was happily swimming.

"You silly thing," I said.

Gently, I set him in the sink with the others, then decided to get my shower. I felt really sticky because some of the goslings had pooped on me during the night. They really are such babies!

I stepped into the tub, turned on the shower—carefully. It's like a booby trap, really. Dad has an inven-

49

tion in there, some machine that squirts out soap and then squirts out shampoo. At least, most of the time it squirts stuff. Sometimes, you can push and push and nothing happens.

I turned on the water, pushed the soap button. It worked this time. I lathered myself up, then laughed out loud, because all my goslings came jumping into the shower with me, splashing around my feet.

"Silly things," I said to them. "Do you like soap?"

They seemed to, splashed and ruffled their wings, climbing up and over my feet, bumping each other out of the way.

I reached for the shampoo button, pressed it, but nothing came out.

I tried again. And again.

I couldn't use soap on my hair.

Dad was just too weird. Why couldn't we just have a bottle of shampoo in the shower like other people have?

I tried one more time—pressed really hard with the flat of my hand. That's when it happened. It squirted out, a whole huge stream of it, like a fire hose. Right in my face, right in my eyes! And I couldn't make it stop.

I howled.

I reached for a towel, a washcloth, but couldn't find anything.

Nothing.

My eyes!

I was really screaming then. But I couldn't move. I might step on my goslings.

"Help!" I yelled. "Help me!"

Suddenly, Dad was outside, yelling, too. "Amy! Amy!" he yelled. "What's the matter? What is it?" He began banging on the bathroom door. "Amy, my god, Amy, what is it?"

I couldn't stop screaming.

My eyes.

Then I heard Susan yelling my name, jiggling the door handle. "Open the door, Amy!" she yelled. "Open up."

"I can't!" I yelled back.

That's when I heard the door splintering, cracking. In a minute, the door came crashing in, and Dad and Susan came flying in behind it.

I was standing there naked and sobbing and rubbing my eyes, and Susan grabbed a towel and wrapped me up in it, but I still couldn't stop screaming. Then I noticed somebody else—this guy, this strange guy!—was in the bathroom staring at me, and I was still screaming.

"Uh, oh," Dad said.

"Get out!" I yelled at him.

"The shampoo," Dad said. "The compressor must have exploded."

Susan was holding me, wiping my face, cuddling me in the towel. Dad was looking sheepish. He turned to the strange guy, and both of them shrugged.

"Get out!" I yelled again. "Get out!"

He did. They did. Susan slammed the door behind them—what was left of it. She turned to me then, wrapped me in more towels, wrapped one around my head, wiped my face.

"It's all right," she said. "It's all right."

"It's not!" I said. I began sobbing. "I can't stand it! I can't. This house is full of . . . contraptions. These stupid contraptions. He is so weird. I miss my mom.

I miss my friends. I miss . . . and . . . and who was that guy in here?"

"He's just a friend of your dad's," Susan answered. "They fly together. It's all right."

"It's not all right. He was in here!" I said. "Right in here."

"It's okay. I don't think he actually saw you."

"He did!" I yelled back.

Susan just kept wiping my eyes, stroking my hair.

And I kept right on crying. "And that Glen person!" I said. "Why did he bring him here? He was going to cut their wings off!"

Susan rocked me a little. "Hush, now," she said. "Your dad didn't know. None of us knew."

"He'll come back and get them," I said. "He said he would."

"Amy," Susan said. She held me tight. "Now listen to me. Can you listen?"

I shook my head. "No," I sobbed.

"Try," Susan said. "Okay? Can you try?"

I didn't answer. But I nodded.

"Okay now," Susan said, when I had quieted down. "Now listen to me. I can't ever replace your mom. No one can. I don't want to. But I can be your friend. If you let me. And the first rule of friends is they have to trust each other. Believe me, I won't let anything happen to your geese. And neither will your dad. And that's a promise."

"How can you promise that?" I said.

"I can," she said. "All right? I can. And I do. I promise."

She kept holding me, kept rocking me. And I don't know why, but I let her. She just kept right on rocking me, and holding me, and rocking me. After a while, it actually felt—well, it felt all right.

52

Chapter 8

I wouldn't say that things got good in the weeks after that, but they did get a little bit better. First, the school term was finally over for the summer. No more snotty girls' comments about my clothes and my accent. Another good thing was that—so far—Glen hadn't returned. Also, Susan wasn't turning out as bad as I had expected. She had a nice sense of humor, made fun of herself sometimes, and of Dad and David, too. But not mean kinds of making fun—just really funny.

But the best, the really, really best, was my goslings. They were lively and funny and smarter than anything, and they followed me everywhere. They followed when I walked, they followed when I ran, they followed me up and over stone walls, through the grasses, the marsh, everywhere. They even followed when I drove Dad's ATV, this all-terrain vehicle, like a huge three-wheel bike. Even when I went fast, the geese ran after me. Sometimes they did it in formation, too, just the way they would if they were flying—a long vee.

For weeks we played, all day long. We even swam together in the pond. I was never alone. All summer long, I had company.

Still, I worried all the time. I never knew when that Glen guy would show up again and try to hurt my goslings. I watched for him every single day. Dad said Glen was on his—Dad's—side about fighting the people who had started to destroy the marsh. Instead of helping though, that made me worry more. Maybe Glen would come back, walk around the marsh like he was just checking it out—and then sneak up from the marsh to the house and try again to get my geese. Dad had built a pen for the geese with a lock on it. They stayed there at night now, because by mid-summer they were getting pretty big. I knew they were safe there, locked up against Glen. Still, I couldn't help but worry.

One night, Susan, David, Dad, and I were all sitting in the house talking, Dad playing with this goose feather, flying it back and forth in front of his face as if he were trying to figure something out.

Behind Dad, David was doing something at the computer.

"I have an idea," Dad said, suddenly.

"Uh, oh," Susan said.

"It's about the geese," Dad said, looking at me.

"What about them?" I said.

"They follow the ATV, right?" Dad said.

I nodded.

"Well," Dad said. "Then they might follow my airplane, you know, my glider. You saw it that first day. If I could adapt it with an engine or something then maybe . . ."

I squinched up my eyes at him. "What for?" I said.

"So I can migrate them to the States," Dad said. "South. According to the books, they have photographic memories. If I can get them to fly down there, they should be able to fly back on their own next spring."

I just stared at him. My goslings? My geese? He wanted to fly my geese away?

"No way," I said. "They're not going anywhere. They're staying right here with me."

"Where would you want to take them?" Susan asked.

Dad shrugged. He waved the feather some more, flying it back and forth in front of his face. "Someplace warm. They fly pretty fast."

"Thirty-one miles an hour," David said, looking up from the computer screen. He pressed some keys. "It's an amazing design. They're aerodynamically almost perfect. Even the head is designed to create lift."

Dad nodded. "Lift," he repeated.

I just kept staring at them. My geese? They were talking about getting rid of my geese?

Dad had promised. Susan had promised!

"Bernoulli's principle," David said. "When a gas or fluid passes uniformly over any surface, the pressure of the gas or fluid is greater on the bottom side. Ergo, lift. Ergo, flight."

"I don't believe this!" I said. I could feel my heart thumping hard, feel the hard lump in my throat that comes when I'm angry. I glared at Dad. "You promised!" I said. "You promised I could keep them."

"You can keep them," Dad said, turning to me. "Not to worry. I promised and I'm not breaking that promise. But they won't stay here. They'll fly away on their own. Unless we clip them. Then they'll never fly."

"They're birds!" I said. "They're meant to fly."

Dad just looked at me. "Right," he said.

"Oh," I said. I breathed in deeply, closed my eyes for a minute.

For a long while, nobody said anything.

I opened my eyes, looked at Dad again. "Well," I said, "couldn't they just . . . I don't know . . . just fly on their own? I mean, maybe they'll decide not to go. Or something."

Dad shook his head. "They'll go, Amy," Dad said. "You know that. Sooner or later. If you just let them go on their own, they'll die because they don't know the way. See, Amy, they aren't born knowing. That's why they need parents, to teach them, to lead them. But they don't have parents. So I could try to show them."

I shook my head. "They won't follow you," I said.

"They might," Dad said. He put his hands on the table, leaned forward to me. "If you help me train them."

I just looked at him for a long minute. Train them? Train them to fly away?

I looked away, stood up. "Unh, huh," I said. "This is crazy. You'll just get them all killed."

And I went outside to talk to them, to reassure them. No way would I let them go.

Outside, I walked up the hillside to their pen, undid the lock and let them out. I sat in the grass with them a while as they climbed all over me. It was very quiet out, a soft evening. I scooped Long John into my lap. "You won't go, will you?" I whispered to him. "Promise you won't go?"

But I was suddenly surprised to feel how big he was—how hard it was to get my arms all the way around him. He was almost like a full grown goose now.

56

I let him go, reached for Igor, pulled him into my lap. He twisted his head, looked up at me, like he was asking me something. I stroked him, looked at him, looked at the others. I couldn't help noticing— they were getting bigger, not just Long John, but all of them. A lot bigger already. They weren't yellow anymore, but a kind of soft grayish. Even now, I could see they were trying to fly. Earlier that day, when I had taken them for a run on the ATV, I noticed they half ran, half flew after me. Even Igor had been trying to get up off the ground, although he didn't do too well at it.

I bent over, put my head down close to the whole pack of them. "Do you really need to go?" I whispered to them.

They just pecked at me, made little crackling, rustling kinds of sounds.

"Tell me, do you?" I asked.

I turned when I heard a footstep behind me. Susan.

She sat down next to me in the grass, put out a hand and stroked Igor. She didn't say anything, just sat quietly.

I didn't say anything, either. But after I while, I said, "Do you think they'll fly away?"

She nodded. "They will, Amy. You know that."

"But . . ." I sighed.

"What?" she said.

I shook my head. "Nothing. But what if . . . I mean, what about Dad's plan? You know how weird he is. Can it work? Or will they all get killed? Dad, too?"

Susan laughed. "Amy?" she said. "I guess you could say that over the years, I've developed a pretty good baloney detector when it comes to men."

"So?"

"So," Susan said. "When your dad says he can do something, he usually can."

I stared down at the goslings. "You don't really believe that he can migrate them, do you?"

"It doesn't matter if I believe it," she said. "He does. And he's usually right when he comes up with a plan."

I pushed Igor off me gently, pulled Muffy into my lap.

"Besides," Susan said, reaching out for Igor, pulling him close to her. "What other choice do you have?"

I sighed, looked up at her. "They'll really try to fly away?" I said. "You're sure?"

"I'm sure," Susan said. "And so are you. I mean, unless you keep them penned up."

I looked down at Muffy, buried my face in her feathers. "But they're meant to fly," I said.

Susan didn't say anything.

For a long time, I just sat, thinking. She was right. Dad and David were right. It wouldn't be fair to keep the geese penned up. Not forever, anyway. I sighed. "All right," I said, finally. "You can tell him it's all right."

Because it was. Well, maybe not all right. But it was the way it had to be.

Chapter 9

So that's how come for the next several weeks, we all worked hard, learning, training, teaching my geese to fly away. To migrate. The first thing we had to do was to teach them to follow Dad, just the way they followed me. We had to start, of course, on the ground. I couldn't expect them to fly with him, if they hadn't learned to follow him. It still sounded just too weird to believe that this would work, but Dad was just weird enough that I was beginning to think it might.

So every morning, we practiced.

I would line them all up behind the ATV, and Dad would get on and start it up. He'd start slowly, and I'd run alongside, till all my goslings were running hard after me, almost flying. Then Dad would rev the ATV and I would step aside. And they'd follow him.

We did that for days. They learned really fast, followed him all over, just like they followed me.

By the end of that first week, when they were used to the ATV and Dad, we added something new. Dad had made a recording of the airplane engine—it made a kind of buzzing sound—and we'd play that when he got on the ATV. We figured they'd recognize that sound, and it would help when it came time to fly.

Of course, there had been lots of problems getting a plane that would work—because the glider needed an engine and wheels and all sorts of things to adapt it for a long flight. But Dad and David and that other friend, Barry, the one who had come charging into the bathroom that morning, had finally concocted something that worked—a glider that looked a lot like a tricycle with wings. They had also had some pretty spectacular crashes before they figured out how to make one that did work. Dad didn't get badly hurt in the crashes—at least, he didn't break anything—but he sure yelled loud enough.

Anyway, they had finally built one, and the geese were learning to recognize its sound. It got so that as soon as they heard the buzzing engine noise, they'd line up right behind Dad and take off after the ATV, half running, half flying.

The only one who seemed to have trouble running so hard, and even doing the little bit of flying that the others were doing, was Igor. He kept turning and looking at me, like he wanted me to come along, and I had to keep shooing him away.

He went. But he was awfully slow. And he hadn't ever gotten airborne. I wondered if he'd ever learn to fly.

The others did though. They were all flying, real low-level flying, just skimming the ground.

Finally the morning came when it was time to practice with the plane. Dad didn't plan to go far, just a short, low-level flight, to get them used to it. David and Barry were out there on the hill with him, helping him get it ready. Susan was with me, ready to help herd the goslings along after the plane.

I could feel my heart beating hard in my throat.

Would they do it? Did I want them to do it?

Yes. I did want them to do it. I guess.

I watched as Dad pushed the throttle forward and started the craft rolling for his practice run before we let the geese out. I could hear him shouting to David over the noise of the engine.

"Right around thirty miles an hour, right?"

"Close enough," David said.

Dad revved the engine some more. Within seconds, the plane had roared to life and was racing down the hill, down, down, down, and then, in just another second, it was airborne, flying high in the morning sky. Up.

I lay back on the hillside, looked up into the sky, watched as Dad flew high over our heads. He turned the craft, then waved at us. Susan and I waved back.

I turned then, looked at my goslings in their pen. Every one of them was eyeing the sky, watching the plane, like they knew what this was all about.

I sat up, moved closer to them. "See that?" I said, pointing skyward. "Think you can do it?"

They kept looking skyward, like they knew. Like they really, really knew.

"You can do it," I said. Even though I felt tears come to my eyes, I blinked them away. "You can do it," I told them fiercely. "Remember, it's what you were born to do."

Dad made a low pass, then came in and landed on the hillside, waiting for Susan and me to get the geese herded out to him.

"Okay, gooses." I turned to them. "This is it. First time flying. Getting ready for the big day. Does everybody understand their job?"

They all honked and made their clacking noises at me, like they knew just what I was saying.

"You can do it," I said. I looked at Susan, then looked at Dad and Barry and David out on the hill. Dad gave me the thumbs up. I turned to the pen, opened it, herded the geese out.

"Now line up," I yelled. "Heyuh, heyuh, heyuh! Come on, follow. Hey, hey, hey!" I yelled. "Goose, goose, goose, heyuh, heyuh!"

They all gathered around me, and I turned and ran for the hillside, ran for the plane that was sitting there, the engine buzzing away, waiting for them.

I raced up the hill toward Dad, then turned around and ran backward, facing my geese. They were running along like crazy now, lined up in a vee, some of them already half flying. "That's good, that's good, that's good!" I yelled. "Come on. Heyuh, heyuh, heyuh!"

I turned and looked over my shoulder at Dad. He nodded . . . and very slowly, the plane lifted off the ground.

I turned back to the geese. "Go!" I shouted. "Shoo!" I waved my arms at them. "Fly away!"

They looked skyward, craning their necks upward. Up. Up at Dad in the plane, now almost as high as the trees. Their little wings were flapping and they were running.

All but Igor. He stopped, turned around and looked at me.

"Go, Igor!" I said. "Go!"

Dad was higher now, higher than the trees, away up into the sky.

Up in the sky.

Alone. Very much alone.

Because every single one of my geese was still on the ground. Not one of them had followed. They stood, looking up, anxious seeming, watching Dad and the plane. But they didn't fly up to join him. They just looked.

After a minute, they turned and ran to me then, crowded around me, squawking, honking. Complaining.

I plopped down in the middle of them. "What did you think we were practicing for?" I scolded them. "Bad gooses! Don't you know this isn't a game? You're supposed to fly. Follow. So you can go safely. You want to stay here and have Glen clip you? Or try to fly alone and get lost? Or stay stuck in a pen for the rest of your lives? This is serious business."

They just honked at me some more.

I glared at them, snatched up Igor. "And you!" I said, holding him and staring into his face. "You should have been an example to them. You have trouble flying, even walking. You should have shown them. If you could do it, they'd know they could, too."

Igor just poked his little face in mine.

I set him down.

The others kept scrabbling and honking and jabbering at me.

I shook my head at them. "We're going to try again, you guys!" I said. "Let's see if you can get with it this time."

I waited for Dad to come back in, and when he landed he grinned and waved at me. "Don't worry," he yelled over the noise of the plane. "We'll just try again. They can do it. It's just going to take some practice. Line them up again."

I did, with Susan helping this time. I got them all crowded around me, then began running, harder, faster this time. When I had them going really fast, I turned around facing them. "Heyuh, heyuh, heyuh!" I yelled to them. "Goose, goose, goose, heyuh, heyuh."

Behind me, Dad revved up the engine, and right away I could see the geese look toward the plane, their necks stretched out, eager looking, ready to go.

"That's right!" I told them. "That's the sound. Now follow it."

Up the hill to the buzzing plane we ran, me, Susan, the whole flock of geese.

"Remember that sound!" I yelled to them. "Remember it? Now go!"

Dad took off, up, up in the sky.

Away.

Again.

Alone.

Again.

Every single one of the geese stayed right on the ground.

I just plopped down in the middle of them, too mad at them to even talk to them.

Dad came back in, and we tried again—and again—and each time it was the same. Dad got up in the air. The geese stayed tight on the ground.

Finally, after four tries, Dad was ready to quit for the day.

"I'm not discouraged, Amy," Dad said, climbing out of the plane and walking down the hill to join Susan and me. "We'll try again tomorrow. It takes time for them to learn. They will."

I didn't answer, just shrugged. I felt close to tears.

"I was stuck with Dad. And he was stuck with me."
(Anna Paquin is Amy)

"That's my dad, with these wings attached like a glider
on his back." (*Jeff Daniels as Thomas*)

Amy lifts the eggs, one at a time, from the nest.

"I brought the whole lot of them into the house."

"It's called imprinting." They'll follow her anywhere.

"Dad thought if he could get them to follow
his plane, he would be able to show them the way."

Barry and Thomas work on the ultralight.
(Holter Graham and Jeff Daniels)

Amy and her dad practise flying over and over.

"They wanted to come with me!"

"We had to get them to the Atlantic Flyway in North Carolina by November 1." *(Halter Graham and Dana Delany)*

An entire military base goes on alert.

Thomas tells Amy she must go on without him.

". . . coming down ever so slowly, gliding in.
Into the marsh, into the fields, into home."

Anna Paquin, Dana Delany, and Jeff Daniels star in the film
loosely based on the autobiography of Bill Lishman.

And confused, too. Because before, I hadn't wanted them to go. Now I was worried sick because they wouldn't go.

Silently, I herded them back to their pen while Dad and Susan walked to her car, David and Barry to their pickup truck. I couldn't help feeling discouraged, and even a little mad at the geese. They had to learn to migrate. They had to! What would happen if they didn't follow Dad? How would they learn? What if they really did try to go on their own, and what if they did get hurt or killed—flying into power lines or something? They'd try it soon, too. Just looking around, I could see that summer was full on now, and nights were already getting colder. In no time at all, it would be fall. They'd migrate. Or try to.

Unless I kept them penned. How could I do that to them?

"You really are dumb," I muttered to them as I led them toward the pen. "Glen is right. You are dumb."

They clacked and honked at me, like they were answering, arguing.

"It's true," I said. "And if you aren't dumb, you're sure acting dumb."

I opened the pen door, herded them in. They crowded close to me, swarming all over me, but I was too mad to make up with them.

"I'm not amused," I told them. "This is serious. You have to learn this."

They kept crowding around me, bumping their heads against me, twining around my legs like children.

Then I thought—they are children, my children. And I'm their mother. Even Glen had said it—they imprint on the first living creature they see. So even if they wouldn't follow Dad, they'd follow their mother. . . .

I took a deep breath, looked up the hill at the plane.

No.

Yes?

I turned and looked down toward Dad and the others. David and Barry were already gone. Susan was in her car, and Dad was leaning in the car window, probably smooching it up with her. They wouldn't look up for a while.

I turned again to the plane.

My heart was beating hard, and I felt like I could hardly breathe. Did I dare?

I looked down at the geese. They were still twining around my legs, climbing all over me, like they had ever since the day they were born, following wherever I went.

I took a deep breath. "Okay, you guys," I said softly. "Okay. But you better get up in the air this time."

Chapter 10

I opened the pen, let the geese out, then closed the pen after them. Then I turned and ran up the hill to the plane, all of them following me.

I was a little scared, but not that much. I mean, it was really simple, the simplest thing in the world. You just pushed the throttle forward and the plane went. How hard could that be? I'd watched Dad do it a zillion times.

After you pushed the throttle, it rolled a little, bumped a little—and then it was airborne. You flew a while, pushed the throttle the other way and then came down. No big deal. Even if I did come down hard—so what? Dad had crashed a couple of times, and he didn't break his neck or even his little finger. He just got up and walked away.

I looked down at the geese again, then up toward the plane. Dad and David and Barry had put wheels on the plane so it would land more smoothly. Not only that, the wheels stayed down all the time, even when the plane was flying, so it wasn't even like you had to do anything to put them down. You just flew up. Then down.

I turned around and looked behind me again, down the hill toward Susan's car. Dad still had his head in the car window, his back to me.

My geese were crowding around me, jostling each

other, like they each wanted to be closest to me—or maybe each wanted to have first place flying.

"Think you can do it, you guys?" I said.

They honked, crowded closer.

"Okay," I said. "We'll see. But you better fly this time. Remember what we practiced? Remember what I told you before?"

I had gotten to the hillside, and I climbed the small incline to the plane, my goslings trailing me. I figured we were hidden from Dad's view by the trees, but just in case, I turned and looked once more.

No, I couldn't see him. So he couldn't see me. Of course, once I got up in the air, he'd see me. But by then there'd be nothing he could do about it.

Once at the plane, I stood there studying it, figuring things out. Yes, there was the throttle. And a steering bar. That's all. No other controls, no nothing. How difficult could the steering be? If I could steer a bike or an ATV, I could steer a plane. Right? I took a deep breath, climbed up into the plane and lowered myself into the seat. My heart was beating like crazy, but I wasn't so much scared as excited. I was going to fly. And maybe, just maybe, my geese would, too.

I settled myself firmly in the seat, strapped myself in, then picked up Dad's head gear from the floor and put it on. It felt heavy and awkward, but I thought it best to use it. I'd never seen Dad fly without it.

I looked at the throttle again, then looked carefully out in front of the plane, just the way I had seen Dad do. The grass and hillside were nice and smooth, no big rocks, no nothing. Dad and David and Barry had cleared all the rocks and stuff away.

68

I looked down at my geese then. They were watching me, attentive, focused. Funny, but they were quiet, not calling and honking, like they knew it was time to pay attention, like they knew this was a big moment. Every one of them stood still, just watching me.

"Now follow!" I said. I pointed up at the sky. "Up!" I said. "Ready?"

They made some quiet honking sounds then.

"We talked about this before," I reminded them. "It's what you were born to do."

I looked away from them, concentrated on the plane. I took a deep breath and eased the throttle forward, just the way I'd seen Dad do—slowly, slowly, carefully, barely inching it forward.

It took just a moment, but then the engine roared to life, and the plane began to roll—slowly, really slowly, barely moving at all. I pushed the throttle just a little further. The plane rolled faster, then faster, but still it didn't lift off. I bit my lip, pushed the throttle a little more. Suddenly, the plane leaped forward, hit a bump, bounced, rocked.

I sucked in my breath.

Steady it! How? But there was no way to steady it. It just bounced, bounced again, and then bounced UP. I was up! I was airborne. I had my hand on the throttle, and I was going up, up in the plane by myself. I was doing it!

I took a deep breath, grabbed the steering bar, looked down. I was clearing the trees. I was up, over the hill.

I turned and looked back. I could see them. I could see my geese—they were coming on, coming, running.

Running hard.

On the ground, still.

And then . . . yes! They were flying, trying to. Barely off the ground, but trying, their wings flapping wildly!

I kept watching them, looking back behind me, holding my breath. Yes, they were up now. Yes! Four, five, six, lots of them—they were up in the air now, lined up behind me. In the air, flying, right behind! They were right there, their wings flapping. I could even hear the sound of their wings.

I was flying. They were flying. They were in the air, following me.

I turned front, threw my head back, felt the wind in my face. Yes! I was flying.

I laughed out loud, then yelled, a huge whoop! just like Dad had done that first day. I couldn't help it.

I whooped again.

I was flying with my geese!

I turned around, tried to count them. And then I realized—Igor. Where was Igor?

I leaned out, looked down.

Dad. Dad was running through the meadow, running up the hillside, waving his arms.

"It's okay!" I yelled. I leaned forward, bumped something by my knee. What? And suddenly the engine died. It died. Stopped. And we were going down.

Down. Straight down.

The throttle. Where was the throttle? I reached for it . . . but. . . .

There was no sound, no engine sound, just the whoosh of air, and then silence, except for my heart pounding hard in my ears. Was I going to die?

70

Dad hadn't. . . .

And that's the last thing I remember before the bump, the huge bump that felt like it tore my head off.

When I opened my eyes . . . did I open my eyes? Or was I dead?

Yes, I must have died. No, I was swimming, that's what I was doing, swimming through the air, but it must have been night, because it was dark, all dark around the edges, and the geese were with me, flying in formation, except for this . . . this person, somebody who was holding me, cradling me.

"Amy, oh, my god, Amy, talk to me."

Why was he holding me? I could fly. Swim.

He was holding me in his arms.

"Amy! Talk to me."

I opened my eyes.

Dad. It was Dad. What was he doing here?

And why was he crying?

"Hi," I said.

"Amy!" he said. "Amy."

He hugged me to him. "Oh, Amy, are you hurt?" he said.

"I don't know," I said. I blinked at him. "Are you crying?"

He nodded. He was kneeling on the ground, cradling me in his arms. "I thought you were . . ."

"I was flying," I said.

"Yes," Dad said. "I know."

"You're not mad?" I said.

"You're all right," Dad said. "That's all that matters. You're all right."

Igor suddenly limped up to us, honking, out of breath, worried sounding. He began pecking at me.

"Stop it, Igor," I said. "I'm all right."

I looked up at Dad. He was looking down at me, still holding me, rocking me a little.

"Dad?" I said. "Did you see it?"

"What, Amy?" he said.

"They flew with me, Dad," I said. I realized my voice was weak, whispery, and I tried again. "They flew with me, Dad," I said. "It was beautiful."

"I know, honey," Dad whispered. "I know."

Chapter 11

Next day, Dad tried flying again, but again the geese didn't follow him. He tried again and again and again. We tried everything. But they just wouldn't go with him. He made me promise—swear practically on my life—that I wouldn't try it on my own again, even though I knew I could do it and I knew they would follow me. All I had to do was learn how to fly, and how hard could that be?

But Dad said no. Which I thought was totally mean of him.

I was sad and mad, Dad was sad, David was worried, and Susan was depressed, and I think even the geese were sad. They seemed restless, unhappy, pacing in their cages, honking and muttering to themselves.

Every time I walked into the house or into the workshop or into the barn, somebody was there talking about it—Dad and Susan, or Dad and David, or Dad and Barry. Somebody. They were all talking. And all they talked about was how we'd have to do it. The nearer it got to fall, the more certain it seemed: We'd have to clip their wings.

One night, I went out on the tire swing, swung so hard I thought I could take off into the air, even without a plane. I thought of my mum, thought of home, thought of my old friends. But nothing made me feel better.

I swung harder, talked to Mum inside my head, told her everything that was happening. I do that sometimes, and sometimes it helps. Remember? I told her. Remember how you said that night that I'd be a good mother to the geese. Remember? You said so. But know what? I'm not. At least, I'm not good enough. Because I'm not old enough. And I don't know what to do.

I swung harder, higher. And dumb, but the whole time I swung, I felt like I was waiting, waiting for her to answer.

Sometimes she did answer—inside my head. Like the time she talked to me about the eggs. But this time, she didn't. She wasn't even there.

It was like I was completely alone.

I went back in the house and started upstairs to my room—and stopped dead on the stairs. David and Dad and Susan were having this big fight. David said something about how they could make a new plane, a good light safe one, but it would cost a lot—and Dad was saying, who cares about cost, I'll sell the lunar lander, people have been begging me for it—and Susan was shouting. She really was.

"Tell me you're kidding!" she yelled.

"No," Dad said. "I'm not. See, the birds will fly with her. And she'll fly with me. I could lead them all south."

"You want her to pilot one of those things?" Susan said. "I can't believe you would even consider it! She's a child."

Dad was quiet for a minute, and then he said, "Yeah. You're probably right. I don't know what I was thinking."

"I can do it, Dad!" I yelled. I raced down the stairs and into the kitchen. "I really can."

Dad made a face, shook his head.

"Just give me a chance!" I pleaded.

I looked at Susan, but she wasn't looking back. She was just glaring at Dad.

I turned back to Dad, threw my arms around his waist. "Come on," I said. "This is the neatest idea you've ever had."

Dad shrugged, turned to David.

"We can do it," David said. "We can build a light plane. A safe one. But you better sell that lunar thing, because it's going to cost money. Lots of it."

"I don't care about cost," Dad said. "It just has to be safe."

Susan jumped up.

"I can't believe this," she said.

She grabbed her jacket and purse from the table. "It's the most stupid, irresponsible, hairbrained thing I've ever heard."

Dad held up a hand. "What else can I do? She has to fly them. They won't follow me. It's the only way it will work."

I took a deep breath. Yes! Yes!

"What's wrong with you?" Susan said, whirling around and glaring at him. "You're going to risk your daughter's life for a bunch of geese?"

"I thought you liked the geese," Dad said.

"I DO LIKE THE GEESE!" Susan exploded.

Dad shrugged. "For someone who didn't want to get involved," he said, "you sure are drawing battle lines."

I backed up a bit, looked from Susan to Dad and back to Susan again. This was getting mean. I didn't want Susan to get mad and leave. But didn't she see that I had to fly them? Couldn't she see that?

"You're right," Susan said, pointing a finger at Dad. "I don't want to get involved. I'm not going to stand by your side like the good little woman and say, 'Way to go, Thomas. Put her up in the air.'"

She turned and went out then, slamming the door—and I mean slamming it.

The whole house shook.

Dad and David looked at each other, then at me.

I went and slumped down in a chair, put my hands to my head.

Why did it have to be this way? Just when I thought I might get the big, important thing I wanted—just when I thought I might be able to migrate my geese—something else big and important went out the door. Right out the door.

And up to that minute, I hadn't realized just how big and important Susan had come to be for me.

For a long minute, nobody said anything.

I got up and went to the window, watched Susan practically running down the drive to her car.

I looked at Dad, pointed out the window. "Dad?" I said.

He just shook his head. He didn't get up to go after her. So I did. I ran outside.

"Susan!" I yelled. I raced down the drive to her jeep. "Susan!" I yelled again.

She slowed, then stopped, but she didn't turn around. She just stood there waiting till I caught up with her.

"Susan," I said when I caught up with her, all out of breath. "Susan, I know you don't want me to do this," I said. "But see. . . ."

"No," Susan said, turning to me. "It's not that I don't want it. It's just that I'm afraid for you."

"I know," I said. "But help me. Okay? I'm going to need you."

I came up and stood close to her. I thought of taking her hand, wanted to hold her hand, but decided not to. It would seem too much like I was a little kid. But I did want to do it.

Instead, I stuffed my hands into my pockets. For a long minute, we both stood there, neither of us speaking.

"Amy," Susan said after a while. "Amy, what would your mother say? Have you thought about that?"

I nodded. "Yes," I answered.

"You have?" she said.

"Yes," I said. "I think about what she would say about everything. I think about her all the time. Just before, out in the barn on the swing, I told her everything. About the geese and about them not flying with Dad, and about everything."

"And?" Susan said.

I looked away, sighed. "She didn't answer," I said. "Not this time."

"If she did," Susan said slowly, "what do you think she would say?"

I looked up, smiled at her. "The truth?" I said.

"The truth," Susan answered.

"Go for it!" I said. "That's what she'd say. And know what else?"

Susan raised her eyebrows at me, her head tilted to one side.

"Mum always said friends were important," I said. "So important. Friends help each other."

For a minute, Susan closed her eyes, for a long minute. But when she opened them, she was smiling at me. "You win," she said softly. "I'll help you."

I took a deep breath, smiled back. "Because you're my friend," I said. "You told me you were that day in the shower, remember? You said you were my friend."

"I am," Susan said. "You know I am."

I looked up at her, and this time, I did reach for her hand.

"Know what?" I said. "Mum would like that."

Chapter 12

My dad may be weird, but he's also pretty cool. He can do things faster than anyone I have ever known. And I mean fast.

In just about three days, some men, all dressed up in business suits, came and hauled away the lunar lander. Although Dad didn't tell me what they paid him for it, from the grin on his face, I'm betting it was a whole lot. I did worry a little that maybe he would miss it. He had seemed so proud of it.

He didn't seem to spend time missing it, though. He and David were working on their computer half the nights and half the days, till they came up with a design for a plane for me. I guess they were a perfect combination of talents—Dad with his inventions, and David with his aeronautical engineering. They drew up the plans and bought the materials, and then they built the plane—and it only took a little more than a week for it all to happen. A week of beautiful summer days.

It was a fun week for me. Swinging on the tire swing in the barn, or playing with my geese, or talking to Susan and Barry, or watching Dad and David put together the goose plane in the workshop, I thought that maybe I was feeling okay now—not happy exactly, but better than I'd been in a long time. I also watched Dad carefully as he worked, thought a lot about him. About why he hadn't come to see me in New Zealand for so long and how I felt about him now. What did I feel about him? Good, I guess, good but . . . confused. So sometimes, I just had to stop thinking.

Finally though, the day came when Dad and David were ready. They rolled the plane out of the workshop onto the hillside, and even though I had watched them build it, still, seeing it out there on the hillside—well, it was spectacular. I mean, a miracle. It even looked like a goose, painted with goose designs on the sides, and with a goose head, and the wings were made to look like goose wings. It was just beautiful. My geese would love it, they'd have to love it, I was sure. I don't think I'd ever been so excited—and maybe nervous. Though, of course, I didn't want Dad to know about the nervous part.

Dad had also added all sorts of safety things to it—steering and communications stuff and landing stuff and a fuel gauge—all kinds of things.

"Okay, Amy," Dad said, that first day, helping me into the plane. "We're going to do this very slowly. Okay?"

"Okay," I said.

"First, the goggles," Dad said. "Then the helmet."

I put on the goggles Dad had bought me, and then he handed me this helmet he had had specially made for me, a helmet with a mike attached. It felt weird, but not as heavy as his had that other time I wore it.

"Now watch this," Dad said. "The mike cord goes from the helmet to this plug here."

He leaned over and plugged it in for me, into the radio set on the cross bar.

"Okay?" Dad said. "You don't even have to hold it. Just speak into the mike on the helmet, and it transmits to my plane or to Barry or David on the ground."

"Got it," I said.

"Okay," Dad said. He climbed into the plane, sitting behind me, with his legs around me. "And these are the controls," he said, reaching around me. "Couldn't be easier."

He pointed out the little starter button. "When you push this, the engine starts. When it gets revved up fast enough and you lean into the bar, it lifts off."

"Simple," I said.

"But we're not leaning into the bar yet, not going up yet," Dad said. "First, steering. This is what we're going to practice."

"I already know," I said. "I tried it on yours."

Dad laughed. "And almost killed yourself. Now listen, it's really simple. You just work the crossbar in front. Lean to the left, the plane goes left, lean right, the plane goes right. Lean right, go right, lean left, go left. Got it?"

I nodded. "Got it," I said.

"Now just practice," Dad said. "And I'm right behind here if you need help."

"I won't need you," I said. But secretly, I was glad he was there.

"Ready?" Dad said.

I was. I looked all around. We had like a whole committee on the ground there, watching—David and Barry and Susan. They all looked like proud parents—especially Susan.

I gave them a wave, then pushed the starter button, and the plane began to roll.

"Okay," Dad said. "Lean left! Turn left. We're just running along the ground. Lean right, go right."

I did just what he said, concentrating hard. We were going slowly, but even though it was slow, it was great fun.

I looked behind at Dad and grinned.

He grinned back.

We practiced over and over, lean left, go left, lean right, go right, taxiing slowly.

"Just remember, Amy," Dad said from behind me. "You got thirty feet of wing span here. You have to allow for that. It's a little like having wide hips."

We practiced for a long while, just taxiing along, me learning the way to turn right, left, allowing for wing span. I was concentrating really hard. And it was fun. But I couldn't wait to get up in the air.

Not yet, though. Practice, practice, practice, Dad said. So we did. We practiced. And practiced. For days.

On each of the days, Dad's friend Barry was out there watching, and he gave me a big grin and a thumbs up, every time we went by. He was really awfully cute, but I don't think he really noticed me much, not as a girl, anyway. He probably thought I was just a little kid.

I couldn't believe how excited I was. But I was getting anxious, too. Anxious to get it up in the air, to fly. And anxious because it was getting to be late summer. Other geese would be on their way soon. Mine might try to do the same.

Finally the day came I'd been waiting for. We had been practicing for hours, Dad in the seat behind me, just like the other days.

Suddenly, he said, "Now lean into the bar, Amy.

Lean into it. When you push forward, it will lift."

"We're going up?" I said.

"We're going up," Dad said.

I took a deep breath, felt myself scrunching up my face, the way I used to do when I was concentrating on my music. Lean into the bar.

"That a girl, Amy," Dad said. "That a girl. Lean hard!"

I leaned hard.

"Harder!" Dad said.

I did. Leaned harder.

"I can feel it!" I shouted. "We're going up!"

"Good girl!" Dad said. He patted my shoulder. "We're going up."

And we were! We were up.

"Now remember what you practiced," Dad shouted over my shoulder. "Lean left, left now!"

I did.

"Keep leaning," Dad said. "Make a huge circle of the field."

I did.

"Now go right," Dad said.

I leaned right.

"You're doing it yourself, Amy!" Dad shouted. "I'm not doing a thing. You're doing great."

I could feel this smile growing. I was doing it. I was. I was flying. And soon—soon, I'd do it with my geese.

We flew a long while, and it wasn't at all hard. I had been practicing for so long on the ground, that it felt natural, like I'd been doing it forever. I could just hear Dad's words—even when he wasn't talking—lean left, go left, lean right, go right, lean forward, go up.

83

I flew for a long time, Dad behind me, encouraging me, teaching me. The whole time we flew, I was thinking—thinking about my geese.

I knew they were watching me from their pen. I bet they were looking up, ready to fly with me, just like they were that last time, maybe stretching their wings. Soon, I told them, talking to them inside my head, just the way I talk to Mum. Soon, we'll go. I'm going to fly you away south so you can learn, so you can be safe. Then, come spring, you'll come back to me. We're going to do it. We are. You just wait and see.

Chapter 13

It had come. The day had come. The day Dad said I could fly by myself. I was so excited I could hardly stand it. A little scared, too.

I had a feeling Dad was scared, too, though he tried not to show it. He helped me climb into my plane, adjusting my helmet, my mike, talking the whole time.

"Now remember, Amy," he said. "Lean forward, but not too. . . ."

"I know, Dad!" I said.

"Yes," he answered. "But this time it's going to be different. It's going to be a lot lighter without me on board. So you're going to get lift faster. And you're going to go faster. So adjust for that, right? You won't need to lean so hard into the bar."

I nodded. "I promise," I said. "I'll remember. I'll be okay."

Dad looked at me for a long minute, then smiled. "I know you will," he said. "Now I'm going to be alongside in my plane. I'll be right there. We're going to taxi, then fly. I'll be a little to the side and ahead of you, just the way it'll be when we migrate them. I'll navigate, you follow. Ready?"

"Ready," I said.

Dad went and got into his plane, and when he did Barry came over to me.

85

"Know something, Amy?" he said, reaching in and adjusting my mike cord for me. "I'm a flyer, you know that. And I've been around a lot of good flyers before—but you know what? I've been watching you, and I think you're a natural."

"I am?" I said. "You really think so?"

He nodded. "Some people just are when it comes to flying. I think you're one of them."

"Thanks," I said.

I looked down at the controls, because I could feel myself blushing. Barry liked me! And then I thought, dummy! He just thinks you're a good flyer.

I kept staring at the controls, pretending to be checking my equipment again. Then I heard Dad's voice coming through the mike.

"Papa Goose to base," Dad said. "How do you read?"

"Five by, Papa Goose," Barry answered, speaking into his hand-held mike. "Stand by."

"Can you hear me, Mama Goose?" Dad said, speaking to me then.

"I can hear you," I said.

"Let's taxi a bit," Dad said. "Get the feel of how much lighter it is."

Barry backed away from the plane then, and I started it up and began taxiing, following Dad, remembering to feel the plane, how light it was, remembering to look at Dad, remembering how big my wings were. There were lots of things to remember, but I did. I didn't forget even one single thing.

"Got the feel, Mama Goose?" Dad's voice said after a little while.

"Got it," I said.

"Okay then, let's stop, get in position to go up,"

Dad said. "And when we get up, I just want you to circle the field. That way, if your engine conks out or something, you'll just glide right down here. Don't go anywhere else, right?"

"Right," I said, and I rolled to a stop.

Dad did, too. Then, when we were both in position, he said, "Ready? I'm lifting off. Then you."

I took a deep breath and felt like my heart would burst. I was going to fly. I was! Alone!

I looked over at Susan, at Barry, at David. They were all there, and, of course, so were my geese. My geese were locked in their pen though, because we didn't want them flying after me—not yet. Not till I got more used to this, anyway.

Susan gave me a thumbs up.

Then I hit the starter button and felt the engine come to life. I watched Dad roll, then lift off. Up into the sky.

Then it was my turn.

I was rolling down the little meadow, rolling, rolling. I was picking up speed, faster. Faster.

I hit a little bump, and I remembered that other time, the first time when I crashed, but it straightened out. I rolled faster, and then I leaned into the bar and, with a little more of a bump, I suddenly sailed into the air.

Up. Up!

I was up. In the air. All by myself.

Dad was ahead, I could see him, turning, looking at me.

I was flying. All by myself. High in the air.

I grinned, straightened in my seat.

Flying! I was flying!

I took a deep breath, looked around. Dad had

said to circle the field, low shallow turns. I leaned into the bar, not too hard, just a shallow turn. This was so cool!

"Hello, base," I said into my mike. "Hello, Papa Goose. This is so cool!"

There was no answer.

"Hello?" I said again. "Hello, Daddy, can you hear me?"

Still no answer. Where was he?

I looked around, saw him, saw his plane flying a little in front, a little above. He was waving at me, signaling something.

I frowned at him. Why wasn't he using the mike? Had he forgotten?

"Can you hear me?" I said into my mike.

He didn't answer, just kept waving, pointing. I looked over my shoulder, where he was pointing. And screamed. I couldn't help it.

Long John! Long John was right on my wing.

Long John and . . .

I looked behind.

The others! All the others. They were spread out behind me, a huge flowing line, so close I could hear the beating of their wings.

Oh, God! Dear God!

They were so beautiful. I felt tears . . . not sad, though.

Suddenly, Dad appeared closer to me, on my left, the other side from Long John.

He was frantically signaling something, pointing downward, pointing to his radio cord.

I looked at mine.

No wonder I couldn't hear him! My cord had come loose.

I quickly plugged it in.

"Daddy!" I shouted. "Daddy, look at them. They're flying, they're really flying with me. What happened?"

"I see!" Dad answered. "I see, Amy! They sprung the coop! They wanted to come to you."

I looked away from Dad and toward the right wing. Long John was close, so close I could almost reach out and touch him. "Hi, Long John!" I yelled. "We're flying! You broke out! You came to me."

He moved even closer, and . . . can geese smile? Because he did, I swear he smiled.

Through the mike, I could hear David. "It works!" he was shouting. "I can't believe it."

Then Dad came through again. "Okay, Amy," he said. "Start a turn to your left. Let's see how they follow. I'll stay on your wing."

"I read you," I said, and then slowly began my turn.

I kept looking to the side. Yes, Long John stayed tucked up tight.

And then—why did they do that? Suddenly, the other geese were in FRONT of me.

"Dad!" I said. "They're not very good at it, are they?"

Dad laughed. "There was a time, Amy, you weren't very good at walking."

"Hey, guys!" a voice said, Barry's voice. "You have an unhappy little goose down here."

I turned around, looked back.

The geese were behind me again. Except for one. Who else? "Oh, no, Dad!" I yelled. "We forgot Igor!"

"Let's go get him," Dad said. "Make a slow pass. It'll be good practice."

Carefully, concentrating hard, I made a long, slow turn. I kept checking my geese. They were following—sort of.

"Don't let your speed bleed off," Dad said. "Keep the nose up. Hold that."

I held it, like Dad said. I was way down then, just passing low over the ground.

I saw Igor—saw him looking up. Saw him running.

"Come on, Igor!" I yelled. "Come on."

"Go, Igor!" I heard David yell. "Go."

"You can do it!" Dad was yelling at him.

He was running harder then, harder. And suddenly, his little butt popped up into the air.

"He's flying, Dad!" I yelled.

"Yea!" Dad answered back. "Yea, Igor! Now that we're all here, let's practice. Come on, come back up, and then let's do some turns. Nice and shallow now."

I took them back up, banked carefully, slow and easy.

I kept checking them. They were following, they were. And beautiful. Spread out in a long vee behind me.

I took a deep breath, felt those strange tears again, but all the while I was smiling. I felt like . . . like maybe my heart was flying, too.

And I felt pretty sure that my mother was smiling, too.

Chapter 14

It seemed time flew—and stood still at the same time. Fall came and school opened again, and although I didn't like it any more then than I had last June, still I had to go. One of the worst parts was that we were studying conservation—and that awful Glen actually came and spoke to our class every Tuesday. Like he knew anything at all about animals or birds! Well, I had to be there, but I didn't have to listen to him. Instead, I studied the other girls. They did dress differently from me. Some of them had earrings—and some of them even had nose rings.

I wondered if I dared do that? Then, one day after school, Barry actually helped me do it—not really pierce my nose, just clip on a ring. Somehow, after that, I felt different—more like me, even though I looked more like the other girls.

How come? I couldn't figure it out. But that's the way I felt.

The much more important thing was happening outside of school: We were getting the geese ready. Every single day we flew them, before school, after school, on the weekends, every chance we got.

We had to keep working them until the very last minute, to make sure they were strong enough for the trip. They had to be able to fly two hundred miles every single day. And they had to be able to do it for four or five or even six straight days, depending on our route.

They were getting stronger at flying, we could all see that. All but Igor. He was impossible. He kept falling, bumping into things. And he was always the last one up in the air, and the first one to poop out. I worried a lot about him.

There were lots of other worries, too—like where we were going to take them. Dad and David and Barry knew this guy, Dr. Killian, the birdbrain man, they called him. He's the one who told them about a site where we could take them. It's along the Atlantic Flyway in North Carolina. There were once so many geese flying there, Dr. Killian said, that the sky would be dark with them during migration time. But not anymore. Too many hunters. Not enough marsh land left, encroachment by people. If we could get them to the marsh there, Dr. Killian said, it would be a safe place for them—if we could do it in time.

That was the last big problem: We had to get the geese down there by November 1, because that was the day the conservation law protecting the land would run out. In other words, Dad said, the developers would start the bulldozers, just the way they had in our marsh. And my geese wouldn't have a home there, either.

It was a tight time schedule, but we thought we could do it.

In the planning part, thank goodness for David. He was almost as weird as Dad, but he could figure stuff out, almost as good as Dad. He had a whole map laid out, where we'd go, when we'd stop, how many miles in how many days—even a cushion of extra days in case of bad weather. He and Susan and Barry had gotten hold of a boat and a van, a full supply operation. Dad and I would fly the geese, keep in touch by our control system, land at an appointed spot where the others would meet us with fuel, food, everything we needed, acting like our supply base. David said it was more like an army operation—just to move sixteen geese.

But it was worth it, every one of us agreed on that. Dad said if we could do this, then maybe that would prove that we could migrate other kinds of birds—ones that were becoming extinct because they couldn't migrate, like whooping cranes and trumpeter swans. It was exciting and scary, all at the same time, because nobody had ever done anything like this before.

Now we were almost ready. Except for Igor. He was still being a dud.

One afternoon, just a few days before we were ready to leave, I was in the pen, feeding my geese, trying to encourage Igor with extra food, when I suddenly sensed someone watching me. I turned around.

Glen! Glen in his aviator sunglasses, with that smirky look on his face, standing right outside the pen. I had almost forgotten to worry about him. And now he was back.

"They're flying now, aren't they?" he said.

I stood up, folded my arms. "What do you want?" I said.

He shrugged. "Just came by to see your dad."

"He's away," I said. "And he told you to stay off our property."

93

Dad was away—in town with Susan, getting more supplies. And I wished like anything he was home.

Glen took off his sunglasses, stretched up on his toes, looking around. "Where do you keep the airplanes?" he asked.

I squinted up my eyes at him. "What airplanes?" I said.

He laughed. "Come on. I hear your dad is up to something crazy. And who's the other guy staying here?"

Like it was any of his business.

"That's my uncle David," I said. I tipped my head to one side, looked at Glen, the meanest look I could manage. "He's got a black belt. We call him Killer."

Glen laughed again. "Okay, Amy," he said. He put on his sunglasses again. "But I'll see you again. You can count on that."

I could feel my heart beating hard. I stood and watched him as he got into his truck, watched till I was sure he had driven away.

Then I turned to my geese. "Don't worry," I told them. "A few more days, and we're out of here. He won't ever bother you again."

I bent over Igor, gave him an extra handful of corn. "And you!" I said. "I want you to smarten up. I want you to practice really, really hard. You have to keep up with us, right?"

He stuck his face into mine.

Later, when Dad got home and we were getting ready to take the geese up again for our final practice, I told him about Glen. But Dad just said not to worry. We'd be gone in just two days.

We climbed into our planes, got them ready to

take off. We had this down to a system by now. Dad flew to my left, leading, navigating. And I flew the birds. They stayed tight on my tail, sometimes moving up to my wing. Except, of course, for Igor, who turned up in strange places.

That day, we had just taken off, when I got a call from Barry on my mike.

"You've still got one on deck, Mama Goose," he said.

I looked down.

Who else? Igor.

"You better go get him," Dad said.

"He's got to learn to keep up, Dad!" I said. "Goose Ground," I called. "Put your radio next to him."

"I read you, Mama Goose," Barry said. "It's down."

"Igor!" I said sternly. "Stop fooling around. We're leaving tomorrow. This isn't funny anymore."

Through the radio I could hear Igor honk.

I could also see him on the ground—and he hadn't moved.

"Let's go get him, Papa Goose," I said.

I turned, banked, came in low and slow over our takeoff point.

Igor was looking up at me. "Come on!" I yelled. "Do it."

He just kept looking skyward.

"Do it!" I yelled. "This isn't funny."

"Go, Igor," Dad called.

"Igor!" I shouted. "We're leaving tomorrow. You don't want to be left behind. What if Glen caught you?"

Like he had finally gotten the message and was scared of Glen, Igor suddenly did it—popped up into the air, his little wings flapping like crazy.

"He's up, Mama Goose," Dad said.

"I see him!" I said.

I turned, banked, looked around behind me. All my geese were in formation, Igor way behind. But at least he was up.

I turned front again, banked left, then turned for another look.

Gone. He was gone again!

"Papa Goose," I called into the radio. "I don't have him."

There was a pause, and then Dad said, "I don't see him, either. I lost him behind the house. Slow down and start a turn. We'll head back."

"Roger," I answered. "Turning east."

I slowed, turned, a slow, banking turn.

"Not too steep!" Dad called.

"Okay. Do you see him?" I answered.

"No . . . level out, Amy!" Dad said.

I leveled out, banked over the trees that were already turning brilliant shades of red and yellow.

No Igor.

"Wait, Amy!" Dad yelled. "Here he comes."

I was just coming out of my turn. And then— bump! A bump on my wing.

I turned, looked. Igor. He'd flown right into the wing! Suddenly, all I could see was feathers. Goose feathers flying—and Igor plummeting to earth.

"Dad!" I yelled. "Dad, I hit him. Daddy, I hit Igor. He's down."

I began to cry. I started to bank, turn back. "Daddy!" I yelled.

"Amy!" I heard Dad's voice, stern, hard. "Amy, listen to me," he said. "Look behind you."

"What?"

"Look behind you!" he said again.

I turned, saw my geese, a whole long line of them, flying hard on my wing, trailing out behind me.

"I see them," I said, crying. "So?"

"You have to take care of them, Amy," Dad said. "Get them home. Turn and go home. Now. Do you understand? They need you."

Yes. I understood. They needed me.

I was crying. But I did it. I turned.

And they followed me home.

All but Igor.

Chapter 15

For the rest of that day, and half the night, all of us—Barry, Dad, David, Susan, me—trudged around looking for Igor. We dug through the pine barrens, and through the woods, and every place we could think of that was anywhere near where he fell.

But nothing. Not a single thing.

Barry said that was good. "No little corpse, Amy," he said.

But that didn't comfort me much. What if a creature had gotten him? Killed him, eaten him, dragged him away?

I was sick with worry.

Dad wasn't too encouraging, either. "I have to be honest, honey," he said, as we tramped through the swamp. "He fell from a long way up. I don't want you getting your hopes up."

Hopes up? What hopes? I was heartbroken.

We had been searching for hours, and it was almost pitch dark by then. I could feel the tears coming, feel the lump in my throat.

Susan reached out, pulled me close to her. She held me for a moment, like she had that time in the bathroom.

And that's when I heard David speak, heard this tone of voice I'd never heard him use before. There was something in his voice kind of like . . . well, like awe.

"I don't believe it!" he was whispering. "I don't believe it."

"What?" I said.

I spun around, looked where he was looking. He was shining his flashlight down into the marsh, and as he did, suddenly, there was this loud honk!

Then Igor appeared, trudging out of the marsh, limping, honking, squawking.

"Igor!" I shouted.

I ran to him, bent and hugged him, looked closely at him.

He honked again, loud, complaining—like he was asking, what took you so long?

Igor! And all in one piece. It was really, really Igor.

I looked up at David, at Dad. "Is he all right?" I said.

Dad crouched down, felt Igor's little body all over, looked him over carefully.

"Seems to be all right, Amy," Dad said. "He's lost some of his primary feathers. But that's all right, they'll grow back."

"He won't be able to fly anywhere though, will he?" Susan said, bending over him. "At least, not this fall."

"We can't leave him, Daddy," I said, looking up at Dad. "He's got to go with his brothers and sisters."

Igor honked again, loudly.

I scooped him up in my arms. "He's got to."

"It's all right," Dad said. "Let's get him home. We'll think of something."

I stood up, Igor held tight in my arms. "Don't worry," I whispered to him. "We won't leave you behind. Dad will think of something."

And he would. I knew he would.

I carried Igor home, holding him close to me, feeling the warmth of his little body next to mine as we all trudged back to the house, me leading. I knew it must have been scary for Igor, crashing to earth like that, being lost in the marsh for hours, so I talked to him the whole way home, reassuring him.

"Wait till the others see you," I told him. "They've been worried, too. I've been worried. But you're all right now. And we'll figure out a way to fly you south. Don't worry your little head."

He honked a soft little honk, like he knew exactly what I was saying.

I buried my face in his neck. "You really are a pain, you know," I said. "But I love you anyway."

He honked again, louder this time. Well, at least his honker wasn't broken.

The others went on to the house, and I went up the hill to the pen, Igor in my arms, shining my flashlight to light the way.

It was quiet up there, the night silent and still. A sharp little breeze was blowing, and I could hear leaves shuffling and muttering in the wind. Fall was here. And my geese would leave.

Tomorrow, all would be ready.

"You'll fly away home," I told Igor. "All of you. And then, come spring, you'll fly back. To me."

It was quiet up the hill by the cages, the geese unusually quiet. Maybe they really were worried about Igor?

I shone the flashlight on the cage door. . . .

After that, all I remember is that I was screaming.

I was screaming.

Because the cages were empty.

The cages were empty, and my geese were gone.
Gone! They were gone!

I raced back to the house, burst into the kitchen, Igor still in my arms. "They're gone, Daddy!" I sobbed. "They're gone."

After that, I just remember crying, and Susan was holding me. And Dad, after first racing out to check that I wasn't imagining it—was calm. Calm as could be, he and David, too.

They were already cooking up a plan.

"Now listen, Amy," Dad said, sitting me down at the kitchen table. "First thing, the lock was snipped with cutters. So we know Glen has them. They didn't leave on their own, and no one else would take them."

"He's going to clip them!" I cried.

Dad shook his head. "No way. It's a much bigger job now that they're big. He'd need several people to help him, to hold them. And because he's got this Animal Protection Program or whatever it is, he's got to obey all the laws. It will be days before he can do anything like that. He probably has to check them out first, be sure they don't have parasites, all kinds of things. Trust me."

I just shook my head at him.

He reached across the table, took my hands. "Amy," he said. "I told you to trust me that I would let you keep them, didn't I?"

"So?" I said.

"And you trusted me to help fly them away, didn't you?" he said.

I nodded.

"So trust me on this one, too," he said. "I know what I'm talking about."

"Okay," I said. "But how?"

"We're working on it now," Dad said.

And we did. Half the night we sat up, planning.

Finally, I fell asleep at the kitchen table, and Susan, after a while, helped me up to bed.

By morning, Dad and David and Barry had come up with a plan.

There were so many phases of it though, that it hurt my head to think about it. First, Barry and David had checked in the middle of the night, and yes, my geese were penned in, all of them—all but Igor, of course—behind the Animal Control Office by the lake.

It made me so mad, but Dad kept saying to be calm. We'd do it. Besides, Dad reminded me, next day was Tuesday—Glen's day to be at my school. If he was in my school, Dad said, he couldn't be at his office.

"But Dad," I said. "There's another guy in the office there. You told me that yourself."

"Not to worry," Dad said. "We have a plan. All you have to do is know your part."

And my part was easy. Fly my plane over, be there when Barry and David got the geese loose, fly over till the geese saw me, till they joined up with me. And then head out. Over the lake.

Head south. The first day of our migration.

When Dad told me how Barry and David were going to spring the geese, I had to laugh. It was a wonderful plan. It was so daring that if I didn't know Dad by then—if I only knew him the way I'd known him when I first came here—I'd have said, never. No way. Don't even try. But I was beginning to think now that nothing was too weird—or too complicated—for him to try.

Not only that, he made it sound so simple that I

actually began to believe it would work. And that part worried me a little—that I was beginning to think like Dad, believe in him.

At least, I almost believed.

Chapter 16

Next morning, Susan was ready with the little boat and van and supplies, David had all the camping gear and stuff he had to take down into the states for us, and Dad and I had our planes fueled up. Everything was in place.

Everything but my geese.

There was just one more thing left to do though, before we left to rescue them and migrate them: We had to find a way to bring Igor along.

I'm the one who thought of it. It was so simple— and I knew it would work. I used the snuggly, the one I'd put all the geese eggs in that night I had carried them up from the marsh. With Igor inside, wrapped up tight, wings and all, he wouldn't even try to fly. Not that he tried much anyway, but just in case, he would be safe with me. Snuggled up right behind.

When I climbed into my plane with Igor, my heart was beating like mad, pounding so hard I could hear it in my ears. Could Barry and David really pull this off? Even if Glen was out of the office? And would my geese fly up to me? Could they still fly? They hadn't been clipped yet?

There were so many worries, but when it was time to go, Dad didn't seem worried at all. He gave me a big hug. "It's going to be fine," he said. "We're heading south. You can do it. I know you can."

I made a face at him, but I had to smile. I had this funny thought in my head that any minute now he'd say: It's what you were born to do.

Then we said good-bye to Susan who would follow in the van, got in our planes and took off. Dad led, climbing his plane out and over the town, over the lake, and I followed, just off his wing.

The Animal Control Center was right by the lake, so we did some long loops out over the lake, waiting. Watching.

Every third loop or so, I'd circle closer to land, not too close, just close enough that I could see.

Way down, way, way down in the distance, I could see small figures at the Center—a van and some people. Barry? David? That officer, the one who helps when Glen isn't there?

And I could definitely see the pens.

Even from that high up, over the sound of the engine, I imagined I could hear my geese honking, calling to me. I knew for sure they could hear my engine. I knew that they knew I was there.

I made another slow, wide loop, looked down at the center again. For the first time, seeing the figures down below, seeing the goose pens, I began to smile—to believe that it WOULD work. And I laughed, knowing what was going on down there.

David was going in, telling the officer that he'd captured some wild ferocious animal in the woods, and would the guy please come out and look at it.

Then, when the officer did come out, David was going to pretend that the creature had escaped, and they'd have to look for it. And it was super dangerous, and they'd have to be careful . . . and all the while that they were poking under bushes and around the parked cars looking, Barry would be around back of the Center, using bolt cutters to cut the locks on the pens.

It was taking a long time down there though, longer than I expected. I was beginning to get worried again.

"Dad?" I spoke into my mike. "Dad, what's taking so long?"

"Don't worry, Amy," Dad said. "You know the plan. And you know David—he'll pull it off. He'll look all sleepy and confused and the guy will buy it all."

"Yeah, Dad, but what if the guy's smarter than we think?"

Dad laughed. "Smarter than David?" he said.

I had to laugh at that. Dad was so right. Hardly anyone was smarter than David, except maybe Dad. David acted sleepy and dull, but his brain was always working.

"But it's taking so long," I said.

"Amy," Dad said. "Look."

I did. Looked down.

There. There! David—no, Barry—was working on the pens.

David and the officer were gone around the other side of the building. I could see them, small dots of people. Looking for the escaped wild creature. And Barry was alone by the pens.

"Get ready, Amy," Dad said.

"Roger," I answered. "Going in."

I headed off the lake, and began circling close, as close as I dared. I flew one long, slow, banking turn, till I was right above the center, till I was looking right down on Barry.

I was so close I could see my geese looking up, looking up at the sound of my engines.

Barry didn't look up though, just kept working with his cutters.

I backed off a bit, giving him time.

"Dad?" I said. "What do you think?"

"Go back in, Amy," Dad said. "Try it now."

I did, came back in, a slow, low turn, right above them. Barry must have done it, because suddenly my geese were streaming out of the cages, flapping, scrabbling, stretching. But not flying.

For one awful moment, I thought: They've been clipped!

But it was all right, they were all right, because they were suddenly flying out, climbing out, streaking into the sky. They had seen me, heard me, and were streaking into the sky right after me. First one, then another, then another and another.

I turned away, grinning, climbed slowly, looked behind.

Yes! They were forming up behind me.

I made a long turn, letting them all catch up. Then I made another sweep, one long last sweep, back over the Animal Control Office, over the cages, looking back, counting.

Yes, fifteen geese, every single one of them.

"See them, Igor!" I yelled. "See them! They're coming, Igor. We're on our way!"

He honked loudly.

"All right you guys!" I yelled to them. "We're on our way. Not to worry, Igor's here, too."

I headed out then, away from the Center, then straight down the main street—right over the school!—and looked behind, and every single one of my geese were tight behind me, on my wing, trailing out in a huge vee, Long John leading.

Dad's plane appeared then off my left wing, and he moved in, leading, heading south, just the way we planned.

I spoke into my mike. "Mama Goose to Papa Goose. That was so cool!"

"Cool?" Dad answered. "I just made a criminal out of my own daughter. Now we're both going to do jail time."

I laughed. "Da-ad!" I said. "Don't be so dramatic."

"Dramatic?" Dad said. "Talk about dramatic. We're just beginning. We have to fly a hundred twenty nautical miles by tonight, cross Lake Ontario, cross an international boundary without a permit—with stolen goods—and we're already behind schedule."

"Dad?" I said, smiling.

"We're on the edge, my dear," he said.

I looked back at Igor, at my geese trailing out behind me. Smiled.

"And loving it," I whispered.

"What?" Dad said.

"Igor," I said. "He's loving it. Enjoying the ride."

He was, too. I turned around, looked at him, all snuggled up there in his snuggly.

"Okay," Dad said. "Now let's begin a slow climb. I want plenty of altitude over the lake."

"Roger," I answered.

Dad began the climb, and I climbed with him. We headed out over the lake, over this huge expanse of blue, so big, so long, I couldn't see its end.

Heading south. Living on the edge.

I looked once more back at my geese. They were

flying in a beautiful vee along my wing, so close, so near, I could almost hear the beating of their wings.

"Going home," I told them. "Going south. Just the way you were born to do."

Chapter 17

We flew through the entire day and into the night across Lake Ontario. I was tired, and I knew Dad was, too. But even more, my geese were tired. I could tell from the way they flew, uncertain, ragged looking. And some of them kept trailing far behind.

The sun was just setting and the dark far shore was just coming into sight, when I called to Dad.

"Papa Goose," I said. "We've got some awful tired looking birds back here."

"Just five more minutes, Amy," Dad said.

And then I heard him call to Barry. "Water Goose," he said, using the name he had given Barry who was in the boat below. "We're flying on fumes here. The headwinds took a lot out of us. I see land. We have to put down soon."

"We haven't reached rendezvous one yet," Barry said.

"Doesn't matter," Dad said. "We have to go down. I'll let you know where."

"Roger," Barry answered. "We'll tie up and wait to hear from you."

"Okay," Dad said. And then he suddenly added, "I think we lucked out! Looks like an airfield. Follow me, Amy."

I followed him, but I was worried. What if we didn't meet up with Barry and them later? How would they find us? We needed food. Fuel. My geese needed food.

I looked at the gauge of my tank, looked around at the darkening sky.

Not only was my tank almost empty, too, and my birds tired, but it was too dark to see really well. How were we going to land in the dark? Wasn't it too dark, even for an airfield?

"Papa Goose?" I said. "Will we be all right?"

"We will," Dad said. "Just stay tight on me. We're going down now. I see the place."

Then suddenly, up ahead, I saw it, too—a long string of lights, brilliant blue lights, that seemed to stretch out forever.

"Daddy?" I said. "What is that?"

Then, on my mike, I picked up voices, not Dad, other voices. "Tower," I heard someone say. "Something peculiar out there. I'm going up."

"Papa Goose?" I said. "Dad?"

"It's okay, Amy," Dad said. "Just stay close."

But he didn't sound okay. He sounded awfully tense.

We were heading down. Fast. Gliding in to land, gliding right in over the brilliant blue lights. Suddenly, on either side of us, in the air above, were two planes—dark ones, ghostly looking, right above us, like they were trailing us, following us.

As we came in, I saw more planes, fighter kinds of planes, those ugly, black silent ones with no markers on them that I'd seen in movies, the ones that looked like black ghosts.

We sailed in, right over the tails of two of them, and I could see there were more, a whole lot of them on this runway.

We had landed. We were on a runway at an airport, down, and bathed in this brilliant blue light, so bright it blinded me, surrounded by planes—planes and men in uniform.

"Dad?" I said into my mike. "I got a bad feeling about this."

I looked behind me. My geese were there, had just flared down to a landing. And right behind them, in the light, came the two ghost planes.

I pulled off my helmet, unstrapped my buckle, started climbing out.

"Don't move!" someone yelled. "Hands up!"

I looked over at Dad.

"Do it, Amy," he said.

He raised his hands over his head, and I did, too.

I looked around. It was so weird. We were surrounded by jeeps, men in uniform, men with guns, and they were all staring at us, surrounding us, guns pointing at us. It was like something out of the movies. Only in the movies, you know it's not for real. This was for real. And I was terrified.

"Dad?" I said.

"Okay. Climb down," one of the men said. "Come with us!"

Dad climbed out of his plane, and very slowly, I did, too.

Dad came over to me, took my hand.

"Dad?" I whispered.

"It's okay," he said. "Just hang in here with me. I think I can talk our way out of this one."

"But what did we do?" I said.

"Don't worry," Dad answered.

Hand in hand we went, some of the men walking in front of us, some behind, some beside. They took

112

us into this big room, an office like, with a huge window that looked out over the runway, a room where this very angry-looking man stood behind his desk.

Even I could tell that we were at some sort of military base, an air field of some kind, and this guy had to be the boss, the General or whatever. He was dressed up in a uniform, with all kinds of medals and stuff on it. And he was mad. I mean, furious. His face was red, and he was pacing. And yelling.

The minute we walked through the door, he swung around to face us, started in on us. "Do you realize," he demanded, "that you put an entire military base on alert? Not only that, you put. . . ."

"But sir," Dad interrupted. "It was an absolute emergency. We had no idea this was an Air Force base. It was either land here, or in Lake Ontario."

The General breathed hard, through his nose, making a snorting kind of sound.

He turned away then, looked out through his window to the runway, where the men with the jeeps were still gathered around my birds.

"People!" he yelled. "Stop playing with those birds!"

The men quickly straightened up.

I looked at Dad, shrugged. My birds looked okay, tired but okay. I didn't mind if the guys played with them.

The General turned back to us.

"We're really sorry," I said quietly.

"Sorry?" The General glared at me, pointing his finger at me. "You put an entire military base on alert," he yelled. "You cause me and my staff a mountain of paper work, not to mention setting two

113

pilots back emotionally about twenty years and you're really sorry?"

I looked down at the floor, then up at him. "We are," I said.

There was this long silence while he stared at me. This long, long silence.

His face was so angry, his eyes little slits, that he scared me. I wondered if he was going to yell again—or put us in jail? He just kept staring at me, looking me up and down. And then, he began doing something with his mouth, pulling it in tight, like he was trying . . . trying not to laugh? Or was I just hoping that?

"We promise never to do it again," I said.

And then he did laugh. He actually laughed.

I looked at Dad and he looked at me, and we both smiled. Just a little.

I took a deep breath, looked back at the General. Was it okay now?

The General just shook his head, but he was still laughing, and his eyes weren't little slits anymore. He looked over at this guy who I hadn't noticed before, someone in regular clothes, standing in a corner taking notes.

A reporter?

The General nodded to him.

The guy nodded back, then turned to Dad and me. "Hi," he said. "I'm from the *Rochester Post Gazette*. I was here doing an interview with the General here, and well, we heard about the unidentified—uhm, thing—coming in on radar. But it seems you're okay so. . . ."

He looked at the General.

"It's okay," the General said. "Actually, if they and

their geese were our biggest headache, we'd be lucky. And you can write that."

The reporter turned back to Dad and me. "Think we could get a picture of you with the General here?" he said.

"Sure," I said. "Dad?"

Dad looked at the General.

The General nodded. And then we all stood together while the reporter started snapping pictures.

After that, the General really acted okay. Maybe he'd just been grumpy because we'd scared him a lot. But after the picture taking was over, he gave us some dinner and a place to sleep for the night, and even food for my geese. And boy, were they tired and hungry. He also let Dad use the radio to contact David, Barry, and Susan and let them know where we'd meet next day, and to tell them we were all right—that we hadn't turned into fish food.

In the morning, we were off.

As we climbed into the planes, the General again posed for pictures with us. Only this time, there was more than one newspaper reporter. There was this TV guy and a TV woman and all sorts of camera types, all of them taking pictures of Dad in his plane and me in the Goose plane, interviewing us both about what we were doing and why. They didn't interview my geese though, which I figured was thoughtless of them, although they did take lots of pictures of Igor in his snuggly.

When they were finally finished snapping pictures, we took off, and once more, I looked back for my geese.

They were trailing up into the sky behind me, and

down below, on the runway, the General and the men were giving us a salute.

I saluted back, then checked again on my geese. Counted them.

"Everybody present and accounted for?" Dad said over my mike.

"I just counted," I said. "They're all here. And Igor's real happy."

There was another sound on the mike then— Barry's voice, coming in from the base. "We're all here, too," he said. "And do we have news for you."

"What's that?" Dad said.

"Just listen to this," David answered. He did something with the mike, and then we could hear voices, TV or radio voices, or something—and at first I didn't get it, but then suddenly I did get it. On the radio, the TV, they were talking about us! About me and Dad and our geese.

The first voice asked something like—but why are they doing it?

Another voice answered, "I told you, Don, I don't know. I just know they made this emergency landing at the base, and the little girl's name is Amy Alden. She and her father are flying a bunch of pet ducks or geese or canaries or something—leading them south. In converted hang gliders."

"That's me!" I yelled.

"Hush!" Dad said.

Then the other voice on the radio made some sort of silly comment about drinking brandy in the morning, and then the first guy said, "Okay, you're never going to believe me until someone else sees it. So look up, New York State. If you see a little girl leading a bunch of geese, call us. Let us know where they are."

116

"Listen to him, Dad," I said into the mike. "We're famous. People are looking to see us!"

"I guess they are," Dad said.

"But I'm not a little girl," I added.

Dad just laughed.

"Why does anybody care, though?" I asked. "I mean, it's not so strange, is it?"

Again, Dad laughed. "Amy, you forget in a hurry. Don't you remember what you told me just a few weeks ago—that this was crazy? That we couldn't do it."

"Did I say that?" I said. And I laughed, too.

I straightened up in my seat then, settled in more comfortably for the long ride, looked at Dad flying up ahead, leading us, flying straight and true to plan, down the Atlantic Flyway to North Carolina. Leading me and a bunch of geese.

I turned, looked behind. My geese looked good, flying straight and strong, trailing out in their long vee behind me. I took a deep breath, smiled, turned front again. We were going to get there. We were going to do it.

Because Dad had showed us. He had figured it out, planned it, had come through. He had showed us how. Just the way he promised.

Chapter 18

We flew the entire day, early morning to sundown almost.

Early in the day, my geese were fine, energetic and strong. But by late afternoon, I could see they were tired. They were strung out behind me in a long, tired vee.

Yet I knew we had to keep going. We had that deadline in North Carolina, in the marsh. One more day till November first—one day or, at most, a day and a half, depending on what time the deadline fell—and if we weren't there by then, we had no place to leave them. They'd be again without a home. Then what would we do? Bring them back to Canada? That would never work. Still, they were exhausted now, and suddenly so was I.

"Daddy?" I said into the mike. "How much further? Everybody is really tired."

"A little over ten miles," Daddy answered. "Not far."

Suddenly, right in front of us, crossing right in front of us, right to left, was this huge flock of geese.

"Daddy! Look!" I screamed.

And then, I saw something else—something that made my heart almost stop beating.

Long John. Long John, who was the strongest, who flew right on my wing, all the time, my lead goose who never let me down—he was going, following them.

118

He had taken off, making a tight turn after the other flock. And more—all my other geese went with him, winging right after him, after the wild ones, disappearing quickly off my wing.

"Long John!" I yelled. "Come back!"

Behind me, I could feel Igor struggling, too.

I looked at him. "Where do you think you're going?" I yelled. I turned back then, yelled into the mike. "Daddy! They're gone."

"I see, Amy," Dad said. "I see them. All we can do is follow them. Turn west, Amy. See them down there?"

I made a sharp turn, looked down below. I saw them, all of them, settling rapidly onto a large pond near a farm house. There were a zillion of them down there already, and the others went streaming down to join them—wild geese, my geese, all of them together. They had all settled into the pond, splashed down in that awkward, feet-splayed-out way that they had.

And that's when I heard shots ring out.

"Daddy!" I screamed.

"Break left!" Dad shouted.

I did, made this super sharp turn.

"Daddy?" I called again.

"They're down," Dad said. "They're okay. I didn't see any fall. Set up a short final to that field at your eleven o'clock. Just do it!"

"Roger," I said.

I did. And I prayed. All the way down, I prayed. Don't let them be shot, don't let them be hurt, don't let them leave. Not now. We're so close. Over and over I prayed it. They can still get lost. They don't understand wild ways, not yet. Please let them get to a safe place.

119

I turned, banked, came in.

Dad was already on the ground when I taxied in, and he joined me at my plane. "It'll be okay," he said, leaning over and unbuckling my seat belt for me. "We'll wait and try and call them out in the morning."

I didn't answer, couldn't answer.

I climbed out, took off my helmet and goggles, then scooped Igor out of the back and stood there, looking out over the pond. There were a zillion geese there, my geese, wild geese, all blended in together. Igor began struggling against me, wanting to join them, I guess, but I held him tight.

I looked up at Dad. "What if they don't come?" I said.

"It might be the best thing for them, Amy," Dad answered.

"But they don't know anything yet!" I said. "You said yourself that they have to be taught. The geese here come from a different place. They'll want to go back there come spring, and then mine will get lost. They might. . . ."

At that moment, there were more shots, and Dad and I both dropped to the ground, Dad grabbing my hand.

"Daddy!" I yelled.

And then—we both saw the hunter at the same moment. Only—was it a hunter? Someone was coming toward us through the field, but it sure didn't look like any hunter I'd ever seen. Whoever it was, he—no, she, an old woman, an old farm woman with curly gray hair—was pointing a gun at us.

I looked at Dad and he looked at me, and we both looked back at the woman with the gun. We scrambled to our feet then, but I left Igor on the ground in his snuggly, hidden by the grasses, just in case she was a hunter after geese.

Seeing her coming toward us with her gun smoking, all I could think was—again. Two times in two days, people pointing guns at us! Just like in the movies.

"Weird, huh?" I said to Dad. "Two times in two days."

Dad just squeezed my hand.

"You people don't give up, do you?" the woman yelled angrily, when she got within shouting distance. "Hunters! You're all the same. Now you're poaching on these geese and coming down out of. . . ." She looked at our planes, this disgusted look on her face. "Out of kites to do it!" she added.

"Oh, no Ma'am," Dad said. "Oh, no, we're not hunting."

"Ha!" she said. She looked at me. "And I suppose you have a gun, too, little lady?" She squinted up her eyes at me.

I blinked at her. "I, uh, no." I shook my head, stepped forward a little, shielding Igor from sight. "No," I said. "I uh, I don't have a gun."

She turned to Dad. "You ought to be ashamed of yourself," she said. "Teaching a little one like that to kill God's sweet creatures. I ought to blow a hole in your liver."

I looked at Dad, took his hand again. Did she mean it? Was she dangerous?

"No, no you don't understand," Dad said, backing up a little. "We weren't. . . ."

"No one kills geese on my land," she said, angrily.

At that moment, suddenly Igor appeared right in front of my feet, struggling out of his snuggly, limping forward.

121

I bent, snatched him up, held him close to me.

The woman stared at him, then looked at Dad, at me. "Oh, good lord!" she said. Then she burst out, "Wait a minute! Wait a minute! I know who you are. You're the little girl with the geese. I saw you on TV!"

"You did?" I said.

"And that's Igor," she said, pointing.

I nodded. "Yes, it's Igor."

"Well," she said. She took a deep breath, suddenly growing much calmer, quieter. She smiled, looked all around, at us, at our planes, then up at the darkening sky. "Doesn't look like you can go anywhere tonight," she said quietly. "Need a place to sleep?"

I looked up at Dad. He smiled. He nodded. "If you put down the gun," he said.

She put the gun down by her side, then turned and led us back to her house, jabbering all the way. "Imagine," she kept saying. "I saw you on TV. Just imagine that."

In the house, the woman introduced herself— Mabel, her name was—and she made up a room for Dad and me to sleep. Then she made food, this huge breakfast, even though it was nighttime, of bacon and eggs and toast and fries, and nothing ever tasted so good.

After we had eaten, and Dad had reached Susan and David and Barry by phone to tell them where we were, we settled down in front of the TV for a while. And yes, Mabel was right—all the news programs had stories about us. I couldn't believe it! They made such a big deal out of it.

We watched for a while, just resting, hardly talking at all. It was so good to just sit. Flying was lots of fun, but it was hard work, too. We were in the air for just hours and hours and hours, concentrating, thinking, being alert the whole time. Even though we weren't working like the geese, we were working. It made me realize how tired they must be at night, having to use just plain wing power.

But there was one thing about flying alone like that—it gave me lots of time to think. And I'd been thinking a lot ever since this morning. About Dad. About Mum. About me, and how I got here, and about my geese, lots of stuff.

I looked over at Dad now. Before, when he'd been talking to Susan on the phone, I'd heard him tell her about the geese being with their wild cousins. Then he said something like, "Tell that to Amy."

I figured I knew what she'd said—it was good for them, good for them to go wild.

"Tell her, not yet!" I had said. "Not till they get to the right place, so they can find their way back."

Dad had smiled at me, like he knew how I felt. And I thought maybe he did.

Now though, on the TV, we heard something—something that made Dad and me both sit up straight, attentive. They were talking about us, about our flight, and this man said, "But now we've learned that there may be a problem at their destination. We heard a report, from affiliate WKMR that condominiums are planned for that site, and the developer starts mowing down the marsh by tomorrow night."

"Tomorrow?" I said. "Tomorrow night? I thought we had a day and a half. . . ."

"Hush," Dad said. He frowned at the TV, looked at his watch calendar. "No, it's tomorrow night," he said.

"Can we do it?" I said.

123

Dad nodded, focused on the TV still. "It'll be hard, but we can make it," he said. "We have to make it. Or they kill the marsh."

Then this Dr. Killian, the bird man, came on, and he was talking about the protection of the marsh, and that this land we were heading for was hallowed ground. "It's the ancestral winter home," he said, "of every goose flying today. It's hallowed ground—if you happen to be a migratory bird. And if the Aldens can do this, maybe they've proved we can migrate other birds."

I looked over at Dad.

Yes. We were a part of something important. Not just my geese, but all geese. But starting with mine. If we could do it.

I got up and walked outside. I walked through the woods and out into the meadow, stood there, looking up at the night sky. It was so dark there in the country, the sky almost black, the stars so low they seemed to hang right in the branches of the trees. I tilted my head back, looked at the sky, the stars, the slice of silver moon.

From out on the marsh, I could hear the squawks and honks and rustlings of the geese.

Come to me tomorrow, I whispered to them. Please come to me. Once we get you there, you can be wild, you can be free. But first, you need to find your way.

I stood for just one more minute, sending them thoughts. And then I went and got ready for bed.

In the room that Dad and I were to share, the light was on, but Dad was already settled down in one of the beds. He was lying on his back, staring up at the ceiling.

I crawled into the other bed, looked over at him. I remembered how I had thought about him in the plane this morning, about how he was making this work. How he had promised. How he had done it. I wondered about him. Did he . . . love me? Is that why he was doing this? Did I care?

Did I love him?

I had hated him when I first got here.

I sighed, pulled up the covers.

"You okay?" Dad said.

"Yeah," I said.

"Don't worry," Dad said. "We'll get your geese in the morning. They'll come to us."

"I know," I said. Although I wasn't sure of that at all. And then, almost without thinking, I blurted out, "Dad?"

"Yeah?"

"Dad," I said. "I want to know something."

He looked at me.

"What happened between you and Mum?" I said.

Dad sighed. "Oh, Amy," he answered. "That's pretty complicated."

"Try me," I said. "I'm a smart kid."

There was a pause, and then Dad said, "What did she tell you?"

"She told me that you were both artists. And that was difficult to begin with, because artists can be selfish sometimes."

"That's true," Dad answered.

"And she said she was homesick for New Zealand. And she needed a city where she could perform."

Dad was nodding, looking up at the ceiling. "Right," he said. "She was right about that."

"And she said," I continued, "that you needed the

farm to do your work. So she said you were both to blame."

"I guess we were, Amy," Dad said. He turned to me then. "But we couldn't have done everything wrong, because. . . ." He smiled at me. "Because we had you."

I took a deep breath, looked away, didn't answer for a minute. "But you hardly ever came to see me," I said, finally.

"Oh," Dad answered. "Well, New Zealand's pretty far away."

"That's a pretty lame excuse," I said.

For a minute, Dad didn't answer. When he did, his voice was odd, distant almost, like he wasn't talking to me, but more like talking to himself.

"It took me a long time, Amy," he said slowly. "A long time to admit that I made a mistake letting you both go. And then, after a while . . . I guess I just buried myself in my work. I was angry and afraid, Amy. Afraid how much I had hurt you."

"You did," I answered. "Because you didn't come."

"I'm sorry," Dad said. He turned and looked at me. "I'm really, really sorry."

I just looked back at him.

"And I'm so glad you're back," Dad said. "I'm so glad. Can you forgive me? Can we maybe . . . start over?"

I nodded, then reached over, turned out the light.

"I think so," I said into the darkness. "I think maybe we already have."

Chapter 19

Next morning, before it was even light, David and Susan and Barry met up with us, bringing their supply van. They got us equipped with fuel and food, and then while it was still dark, we all walked quietly to the edge of the pond.

The sun was just creeping over the edge of the marsh when we got there. I had Igor tucked up tight in his snuggly, and I walked to the pond with him, praying, hoping, talking to my geese inside my head. I reminded them about the flight, the goose plane. Our trip.

"Hey, Long John!" I called quietly. "Come, come, heyuh, heyuh!"

The marsh was still, silent, just the rustling of the geese, and an occasional honk. The air was so cold, my breath came back at me, a white vapor.

But that was all that came back. No Long John. No anybody.

I looked up at Dad, standing by my side, peering hard into the marsh. "Try again," he said.

"Here, Long John," I called again. "Here, Frederica, here Sam."

I listened. Still nothing. Nothing but stillness, and some honks from the geese. Lots of geese out there, a hundred, two hundred. And the ones that were mine were hidden among them. They rafted

127

together, not even turning to look at me.

"Muffy?" I called. "Jeremiah? Stinky."

Still silence. Just more rustles and more honks, and an occasional splash. Lots of geese, all of them packed together on the pond like kids on a school playground. Like kids on a playground paying no attention to their teacher.

I looked down at Igor, turned his head gently so he was facing out to the pond. "Couldn't you help?" I said.

He honked loudly.

And just like that, they came to me. They did! Fifteen geese came swimming out of the pack of two hundred. They came from all different directions, like they'd been hanging out with new friends overnight, not just their brothers and sisters. But they came to me, all fifteen geese! My geese.

I looked up at Dad. "Look!" I whispered. "Look! They did it!"

He smiled back. "Yes, they did it," he said. "Now let's go. A long day ahead."

"A really long day," David said. He looked at his watch. "You have just ten hours to do it. You'll have to stay in the air all day."

Dad nodded. "We can do it."

"Remember, the law expires at five today," David said.

"We know," Dad said. "We're on our way."

We headed for the planes, my geese following, honking and calling loudly, maybe saying good-bye to their new friends. And when we took off, they did, too—flying tight on my wing, flying with me. Following Dad.

128

Up in the air, it was foggy for the first little bit, hard to see. We were near Maryland and Virginia now, still many miles from our destination. Dad was flying ahead and off my wing, the way we always flew, him leading on, navigating.

Suddenly, through my mike, I could hear Dad calling to the base, to David.

"Goose Mobile," Dad called. "I'm having trouble with my high tech navigating system."

"What trouble?" David said.

"Don't know," Dad said. "Going out. Not reading strong."

"Could be batteries," David said.

"Uh, oh," Dad said.

"Dad!" I shouted. "How could you forget batteries?"

"Never mind," Dad said. "I know where we are. We should be right around Baltimore."

"Based on your signal, yeah," David answered.

And then suddenly, we weren't over countryside any longer. We were in a city. I didn't know if it was Baltimore, but up ahead, right in front of us, there were a zillion high-rise office buildings!

"Daddy?" I yelled. "Daddy, watch out!"

"We're okay!" Dad called. "Stay tight to me. We're going right down Main Street."

I followed Dad in, squinting into the fog. We were flying right down a street, right down a main street, between office buildings. Dad, the geese, and me.

I saw office buildings and window washers up high on scaffoldings, and everybody was looking up at us, pointing. And then, Dad turned a corner and I followed, my geese followed—and we were out of there.

"That was scary!" I called to Dad.

"Yeah, but we made it okay, Mama Goose," Dad called back. "It's all better from here on down."

And it was, too, because the sun was beginning to burn off the haze, and suddenly it was a beautiful morning—more beautiful because my geese were flying with me, strong and intent on the journey. Below, I could see horses running on a hillside and the flaming colors of the trees.

On and on we flew, all day. It was late day when Dad called over the mike, "How are you hanging in, Amy?"

"I'm okay," I answered. I looked around behind me. "My geese are, too. Getting a little tired, though, I think."

"We can make it, though," Dad said.

"We can," I answered.

"Papa Goose to Mobile," Dad said. "I estimate arrival at about one hour before sundown."

"Sounds about right," David said. "And exactly one hour to spare. The law expires at sundown."

"We'll do it," Dad said. "We have enough fuel, so why don't you go on and set up for our arrival?"

"Roger, Papa Goose," David said. "See you at Valhalla."

Dad turned and waved at me.

He was too far away for me to see his face, but I had a feeling he was smiling.

I know I was. One more hour. And we'd be set. My geese would be free. And the land would once more belong to them.

We flew on, over the hillside, over the flaming trees. I kept checking my geese, but they were doing just fine. Tired and hungry, I bet. But they were fine.

130

And then suddenly, Dad's voice came over the mike.

"Whoa!" he yelled.

"What?" I said back. "Daddy, what's wrong?"

There was no answer.

I looked ahead, looked for him. "Mama Goose to Papa. What's wrong? Where . . ."

That's when I realized—he wasn't on my wing.

"Where are you?" I cried.

And then I saw it—him—his plane. I was flying right past him. He was spiraling over, out of control, spinning down, down, like a huge kite without a tail.

"Daddy!" I shouted.

I made a sharp turn, turned back, followed his spinning plane. "Daddy!" I screamed.

I shouted into my radio, "Mama Goose to Mobile One, Mama Goose to Mobile! Come in."

But there was no answer.

"Uncle David!" I yelled.

No answer. They'd gone on.

"Daddy!" I screamed.

He was down, his plane was down. I saw it land in a field, land and bounce. It was in a cornfield, broken up, I could see it.

"Daddy!" I yelled.

Nothing. No answer.

I circled the field, saw a place to land, circled again and began gliding down. I looked behind. My geese were flying tight formation after me.

"We're going down," I yelled. "Down. Come with me."

Oh, God, please let him be all right, I prayed, please don't let him be hurt. Please don't let him be. . . .

131

No, he couldn't be.

I flew low over the field, glided in. Over beyond the trees, I could see the wreck of his plane.

Please, God.

I jumped out of the plane, ran toward his, fighting my way through brush and trees and grasses. I stumbled, feeling the branches catch at my legs, my face. "Daddy!" I yelled. "Daddy!"

Then I saw him. He was there. He was standing. Leaning against a tree. Standing.

No blood.

"Daddy!" I threw myself into his arms. "Are you okay?"

He sucked in his breath. "I hurt my shoulder," he said. "I think it's dislocated."

I pulled back, looked at him. "Is it bad?" I said. "Can you move it?"

Dad winced. "I've dislocated it before. It's not too bad. But it does hurt."

Suddenly, my geese were everywhere, checking Dad out, poking and pecking at him.

"It's okay, guys," I said to them. "He's okay."

I looked back at Dad. "Oh, Daddy!" I said, leaning against him. "I was so scared."

"So was I," Dad said.

"What happened?" I said.

"I don't know," Dad said. "My rudder, I think. But I can't go on, Amy."

"I know," I said.

"You're going to have to take them the rest of the way yourself," Dad said.

I just looked at him. "Me?" I said.

"You," Dad said.

"No," I said. "I can't."

"It's less than thirty miles," Dad said. "One hour. You can do it."

"No!" I said. "I can't find my way without you."

"Yes, you can," Dad said.

I just shook my head, felt tears come to my eyes. I couldn't. Couldn't go alone. Without him.

"Yes, you can," Dad said. "You know why?"

Again, I just shook my head.

"Because you're very much like your mother," he said. "She was very brave, you know."

I didn't answer, tears filling my eyes.

He reached out, touched my face. "Amy, she went off and followed her dream. Just like you. This is your dream."

"I know!" I said. "But I can't! I'm not like her."

He smiled. "Yes you are. Nobody helped her. She just did it. You have that strength, too, Amy."

I sucked in my breath, all trembly like. "No."

"Yes," he said.

I looked down at my geese, looked out at my plane. It was my dream. But how . . . how could I do it alone?

"I wish she was here now!" I said.

"She is, Amy," Dad said softly. "She is. She's right next to you. She's in the geese, she's in the sky, she's all around you. She is. And she won't let you down."

I took a deep breath, bit my lip. Was she? Would she? And could I really give up now—when we were so close? Give up my dream?

"But what about you?" I said. "I can't just leave you here. You're hurt! Why don't you come in the plane with me?"

"Can't," Dad said. "Not enough fuel."

133

"But . . ."

"Go," Dad said. He pointed out to the field. "I want you to take that plane, take those geese, and go. Go!"

I waited one more second. "You sure you'll be all right?" I said. "How will you get out of here?"

"Hitch a ride. Someone will pick me up. We're not far from the highway. Someone will be by soon, I bet."

"But . . ."

"Go!" Dad said. "There isn't much time. I'll be all right, I promise. Just follow the river all the way to the town of New Hope, turn southwest, and follow the coast for ten miles."

"How can I find all that?"

"You will. You can see it. It's clear as anything."

And then I hugged him—carefully. And I was out of there. On my own. Following my dream. Alone.

Terrified to be doing it.

Chapter 20

I'd never been so scared. Never. I knew nothing about navigating. I knew nothing about flying alone.

I knew east—it was the other way from where the sun was setting now. And I knew how to find the river, because we had been following it all the way in. But then what? How would I know when I was in New Hope? How would I know one town from the other? How did I know southwest?

Dad had still been calling to me as I ran for my plane, something about looking for vans, TV people, crowds. But would I find it all by myself? How would I recognize it all from so high up? How would I see it all?

I climbed into my plane, put on my goggles and helmet, looked behind once more at Dad—waved, and took off. Heading east. That's all I knew.

I lifted off, high, high over the trees. Behind me, my geese lined up, and in the seat behind, Igor was still tight in his snuggly.

Once up in the air, I never looked back at Dad, at his wrecked plane. Couldn't bear to, or I might go back. But up in the sky, I did look at my geese trailing behind me, a long, strong vee.

It seemed that the stop had been good for them, because they were flying stronger now, Long John leading, tight on my wing.

I wondered what they thought about Dad's plane being gone, if they missed it like I did. Every time I looked to the side, I felt tears fill my eyes.

I flew for a long time along the river alone. How long? I checked my watch. Twenty minutes that felt like twenty hours. Twenty minutes of searching for landmarks—the river, the coastline, New Hope. And then, a few minutes later, I did see a town. New Hope? It was the only town I had seen so far, so it must be. Right?

I checked my watch again. Twenty-three minutes since I'd left Dad. It had to be New Hope.

But which way now? Which way to the coast?

I looked left, right.

Why wasn't Dad here? And where was Mum? Dad promised she'd be here.

I squinted into the distance. Nothing. No sign.

I looked at my watch again. Just half an hour till sundown.

Sundown was the end.

Suddenly, I saw it—thought I saw it. A glimmer, like sun on water off to my left. That would be the coast, right?

I squinted, headed a bit further to my left.

Yes! If I turned left here, the coast would be. . . .

But no. I flew along a ways, but didn't see the coast. And I had lost the river.

I circled the town, came back in slowly, a long slow curve. It was so frustrating!

It was getting darker, almost sundown. I didn't have time to fly the wrong way, and then circle back and go the other way if I didn't find it. I flew right down the main street of the town, a long main street, with just one or two people strolling around.

I was lost! I was so mad I could feel tears, dumb tears. How could I be so close, and still be lost!

When suddenly, down below, I saw something—people, the people in the street of the town—two people, two women.

They were waving to me, like they had recognized me, jumping up and down, waving madly. No. They weren't waving. They were pointing. One of them was making a huge sweeping gesture with her arm.

Pointing to me to go right—not left, right. Is that what they were trying to tell me, go right?

I turned, banked a bit to my right, looked down. They jumped up and down, clapping their hands. Yes!

I gave them a wave, then headed on right. East. And yes, that was the right way, because after a few minutes, there it was—the coastline, the ocean, glistening ahead of me. Follow it. Yes. Yes!

I sank back in my seat a little, felt my breath come easier. We were almost there. I turned, looked out at my geese. They were flying along with me, their wings beating true and strong.

"We're almost there, guys!" I called to them. "You're almost home."

I turned back around, faced front, smiling. Almost home.

And then, funny, I heard something. A sound. A voice? Yes, a voice. And a song. That song, the one that was playing the night Mum died, that sad song that had haunted me for so long. Only this time, it didn't seem so sad, just . . . just haunting.

"Fare thee well, my own true love," I heard. "Farewell for a while, I'm going away. . . ."

I smiled, fighting tears at the same time.

"But I'll be back . . . though I go ten thousand miles. . . ."

Was Dad right? Was Mum here? In the sky. The air. The geese.

Maybe even in the people who waved me on my way?

The song came all the way with me as we flew down the coastline as I kept looking down, looking hard. Then I saw it, I thought I saw it. There! It had to be. It was.

I could see a marsh, see the fields glowing in the setting sun. And in the distance—the TV crews, the cameras, the huge things they put up to mount their cameras on. And the bulldozer.

I looked at my watch.

Five minutes. Five minutes to sundown.

And then . . .

Was that Dad? Was that Dad down there waving his arms at me? How'd he get there so fast? He must have gotten a ride instantly. I shook my head. He was so weird—weird and wonderful and smart—and now I thought maybe he was even magic.

I looked over my shoulder.

My geese were all there—all fifteen of them.

Slowly, carefully then, I led them in, our final approach, coming down ever so slowly, gliding in. Into the marsh, into the fields, into home. I settled my little plane into the field, back a ways from the crowd.

Home. My geese were home. Free now. Free to be wild.

"You're home now guys," I told them. "You're home."

I bent, took Igor out of his snuggly, freed him. His

brothers and sisters came crowding around, honking, fluttering, like they knew where they were, like they recognized home.

Then as Dad ran to me, helped me out of the plane, as Susan and Barry and David hugged me—I began to laugh, even though I was crying at the same time. And I was still hearing that music.

"I'll be back, though I go ten thousand miles. . . ."

"You did it!" Dad said.

I looked at him. "Yes. And you were right," I said. "About Mum."

He raised his eyebrows at me.

I didn't say anything more, because I didn't have to. I knew he knew.

Mum was in the sky, the air, the geese. In those two people who had shown me the way. In Susan and Barry and David.

She had come back. Or maybe had been there all along.

I reached for Dad, took his hand, held it tight. Because Mum wasn't the only one who believed, who followed a dream. Dad did, too.

And he had shown me how.

Epilogue

The next spring, when the tiny pale leaves were just beginning to bud on the trees on the farm, there was a sound.

It came in the night, when I was asleep. But even in my sleep, I thought I heard something. It was small at first, the sound of splashing, like a feathered body thudding into the water, then another, and another.

I turned over, frowned. What was it?

And then, I was fully awake because there were other sounds, honking, rustling. Honking!

I jumped up, pushed aside the curtain.

Yes! Yes.

I started to call, to waken Dad and Susan. But not yet. Not for just another minute.

Instead, I stood at the window, looking out into the still cold dawn. Smiling. Believing.

Because they had returned.

Just the way we believed they would.

Behind the Scenes
with *Fly Away Home*

Top left: Jeff Daniels stars as Thomas Alden. Top right: academy Award® winner Anna Paquin stars as Amy Alden. Bottom left: Carroll Ballard is the director. Bottom right: Dana Delany plays Susan Barnes.

Behind the Scenes
with *Fly Away Home*

(The following was prepared by Columbia Pictures, drawn from interviews with the cast, filmmakers, and Bill Lishman, on whose life and work the movie story is loosely based.)

Creating the Movie Story

Fly Away Home is a fictional story, but the events at its core are grounded in scientific fact and real experience. Thomas Alden, who exists only in the film, has a real-life model in Bill Lishman, the Canadian artist who really did teach geese a migration route. Lishman, with Joe Duff and Dr. William Sladen, working together in Operation Migration, proved that wildfowl can be imprinted to ultralight aircraft and taught new, safer migration routes.

"Migration is not actually instinctive with birds," explains Lishman, "it has evolved over time and the route is passed on from one generation to the next. If a species is wiped out in an area, the migration route is lost with them, so if you want to reestablish that species in that area, you have to find a way to show them the route. In 1993, Joe Duff and I raised a flock of eighteen geese and tried an experiment to fly them to Virginia, and it was successful."

Their widely publicized success with Canada geese offers hope for seriously endangered species such as Japanese red-crowned cranes and the trumpeter swan.

It also offers images of such heart-stopping beauty that they virtually cried out for a major movie to be made. Around those images, two Hollywood writers Robert Rodat and Vince McKewin built a warm story of a father and daughter forging a new life together.

"The story is about a father/daughter relationship and that's nice," says Lishman, "but I think *visually* it's fabulous because it shares that image of the birds, that point of view of flying with them."

Columbia Pictures and producers John Veitch and Carol Baum accepted the challenge of bringing the story and its amazing images to the screen. Having themselves been "imprinted" by Bill Lishman's incredible shots of geese flying only an arm's reach from him, the filmmakers were determined to share with feature film audiences the sense of awe the sight inspires. To do so, they approached the same team responsible for the breath-catching visual glory of *The Black Stallion*, director Carroll Ballard and cinematographer Caleb Deschanel.

"Carroll had also done *Never Cry Wolf*," says producer John Veitch, "and he seems to have a kind of talent or flare for stories about animals and children so we felt if we were lucky enough to get Carroll, we should grab him. I felt that we would be very, very fortunate to deliver the story that Carroll is delivering. One of the stars of our picture is the photography, and Caleb is delivering that . . . in addition to *The Black Stallion*, Caleb had also done *The Natural* and *The Right Stuff*."

"This film is a drama and an adventure," says producer Carol Baum, "It has a child as the leading character, but its classical qualities, hopefully, will appeal to everyone."

Still, even for people possessing uncommon talent, the making of a scripted, feature-length film with a cast of essentially wild creatures is not easy. "There are more

Director Carroll Ballard, Anna Paquin, and a flock of goslings prepare for a scene.

Bill Lishman, the Canadian artist who really does teach geese to migrate, and on whose life and work the movie is loosely based.

challenges in this picture than any other film I've been involved in," says Veitch. "The weather is always a problem. Working with the birds and getting them to work on command or 'hit their marks' like an actor would— we wondered, would they do it? The flying . . . how close would they stay to the planes? We have been very lucky. The geese . . . would follow Anna and the father's plane would take off and they'd stop, like it was on cue, with her, and they wouldn't go any farther."

The fictional characters who live Lishman's dream of flying with the geese are Thomas Alden, played by Jeff Daniels (*Speed, Dumb and Dumber*), and his daughter Amy, played by Anna Paquin (*Jane Eyre, The Piano*), a father and daughter who were parted when the child was very young and reunited by her mother's tragic death nine years later. The story of their tentative steps toward a loving family life provides an emotional counterpoint to the saga of a little family of wild geese, orphaned before hatching and adopted by the lonely girl.

The fictional characters give a dramatic context to the true story of Bill Lishman's activities with the wild geese. "We really wanted to capture the essence of Bill Lishman's character, because he is larger than life, but we had to make a movie of it," says Baum, "so we invented a story about a girl who has lost her mother and who reunites with her father. That is made up. In real life, Bill has a wife and a daughter and a nice family. But when you make a movie, you have to create situations that allow for the growth of the characters."

The dramatic story line was pure invention, but the heart of the film is truth—the geese, and the fact that, despite those who said it couldn't be done, Bill Lishman and his colleagues did fly with the geese and teach them a new migration route.

More about Canada Geese

A Canada goose is twice the size of a seagull, frequents flyways in both Western and Eastern Canada (Columbia shot *Fly Away Home* near Toronto on Lake Ontario), and, when young, can easily be imprinted to a person or a vehicle (car, motorcycle, boat, or plane).

Inclined to form family groups, Canada geese often mate for life, and both male and female are involved in early rearing. Incubation of eggs takes about twenty-eight days, and an additional sixty-three days on average is required for the goslings to be capable of flight. During the rearing period, the adult geese will molt, lose their feathers, and be flightless for about a month.

Wild geese tend to make their migration flights in the cool of early morning and at night, often flying in complete darkness. They are capable of flying through fog, which sometimes makes the human pilots dependent on their charges to navigate and lead the way.

Making the Film

Making this film was, perhaps, more complex than Operation Migration itself. First, a flock of geese had to be imprinted on actress Anna Paquin, who plays Amy Alden. This involved elaborate precautions, including having Lishman's real daughter, similar in age and size to the actress, "stand in" for Paquin while recordings of Paquin's voice were played for the hatchlings until the young performer could arrive on the scene. Then the geese had to be taught, like the real-life Operation Migration flocks, to imprint on the ultralight aircraft that would be used in the filming. And, because geese mature at their own rate, with no regard for a film production schedule, several clutches of eggs, with staggered hatch times, were

147

needed to show Amy with the geese at various growth stages. Initially, about sixty geese were prepared for possible starring roles in the film. Wrangling them was no small job for Joe Duff and his helpers.

"We [Operation Migration] imprint the birds to the aircraft to teach them to migrate, but with these birds, we had to imprint them to the aircraft Tom Alden flies and the one Amy flies, and to our camera ship," says Duff, "For some scenes we also imprinted them to a boat that we put an aircraft and a main actor on. So we've got birds that are imprinted on lots of things, but it's not going to harm them in the long run because the imprinting process is a natural phenomenon that basically expires as birds mature."

The cameras presented a technical problem, too. The original footage of the geese flying with Bill Lishman was shot with a small video camera. A feature film camera is much larger and has a lot more weight. Geese fly at a maximum speed of about thirty-two miles per hour—stalling speed for most aircraft. The ultralights that are used for Operation Migration can fly at "Mach Goose," but they are too light to carry a film camera with its operator, batteries, and film load. A special aircraft, with extra-long wings, was designed that could be flown slowly enough, without falling out of the sky, to capture shots of the flying geese. The only other thing required was the cooperation of a flock of geese.

"When they head for home," says pilot Duff, "the message is clear. It starts with one bird . . . then two more will follow him and the first thing you know, the flock's going *that* way."

The pilots had more than just birds to keep track of. There was also a helicopter in the air, and the ultralights had to be sure they did not venture into the

For some scenes geese were imprinted to a boat carrying an aircraft and a main actor.

wash from its blades. The coordination required was similar to mounting an aerial acrobatics act.

"Before we all go up," says Westcam operator Hans Bjerno, "we have a meeting with the ultralight pilots to let them know what type of scene we will be filming and what we are looking for. Up in the air, we talk to them on the radios, but we work around *them*. In formation flying there's always one person who flies off the other and in this situation, we're always flying off the ultralights . . . we *can't* get in front of them and cause turbulence. The beauty of the Westcam is that we have a long lens on that camera, and it's gyro stabilized, so we can be far enough away and still get a tight shot on a goose or on the formation."

All the difficulties involved in the flying shots were, in the end, more than worthwhile according to Joe Duff, because what the audience sees is very much what he and Bill Lishman see when they fly south with one of their flocks. "We knew the visuals were there," says

Duff. "It is a beautiful thing, and most of what you are seeing in this film is real. It's right there. It happened."

The Cast's Experience

Making a film about flying with a flock of Canada geese made an impression on most of the cast, too. The project offered sights and experiences that don't come along as part of most movie deals.

For actress Anna Paquin, filming offered one new and exciting experience that would be a thrill for most young people. "I think one of the most enjoyable things I did was taxiing an airplane," says Paquin, "but you know, I don't actually get to take off. I do get to taxi it by myself with Jeff [Daniels] sitting in the back. He could actually override my steering and the gas, but he didn't need to."

For Daniels, working with the geese provided a variety of experiences unique in his acting career: "We had one scene with about fifteen little goslings on the breakfast table . . . and they were nipping at my beard, which didn't really happen until we were shooting. You think you've lost your nose or something!

"We had to bond with the geese. You know, it's one thing for Gordie, Bill Lishman's son . . . they'll follow Gordie anywhere, but eventually, Gordie's got to get out of the picture and they have to follow me. So you spend a lot of time making some of the most ridiculous sounds you've ever made in your life, anything to get them to follow you while the cameras are rolling."

Dana Delany, who plays Thomas Alden's girlfriend, Susan, agrees:

"You just have to throw your dignity out the window. There is no way you *can't* look like a fool, because, basically, you have to become a goose. You

Left: Terry Kinney plays David Alden. Right: Holter Graham plays Barry Strickland.

have to get down and make weird noises—you just have to make a fool of yourself."

For Daniels and Delany, as for so many of the cast and crew, enthusiasm for the picture started when they saw tape of the ABC-TV *20/20* television segment about Bill Lishman flying with his geese:

"It just brought tears to my eyes," says Delany. "We all want to be able to do that, and Bill Lishman actually does it."

"It was so moving, you know," says Daniels, "I remember seeing Lishman, on TV, going across Lake Ontario with the geese and saying, 'Whoa! Here's this wild guy, this free spirit with ideas.' It's just one of those roles you want to do, got to do."

"The story is about this guy who . . . won't take no for an answer—so *anything* is possible for him," concludes Daniels.

Like many others, Daniels found moments of pure

amazement in the filming. "We filmed a lot at 'magic hour,' with that orange sunset light, and here comes Lishman over the trees with these geese, and our whole crew—the jaded Hollywood crew—just says, 'Wow. Time out. Look at that.' That's why we're here—to get that on film."

Terry Kinney was drawn to the role of Thomas Alden's brother, David, by a similar fascination with Bill Lishman's story. "I was fairly amazed that this guy dreamed this up and then actually did it," says Kinney. "It makes you feel kind of hopeful about life in general."

Kinney was also eager for the chance to work with director Carroll Ballard, whose previous work had impressed him deeply. "*Never Cry Wolf* was a movie that epitomized filmmaking to me because filmmaking has never been about dialogue for me, it's been about images. That's what he concentrates on. He tells his stories through imagery."

For actor Holter Graham, the role of Thomas Alden's friend Barry Strickland was a draw enough in itself. "I've been cast as a hit man, I was cast as a rock star, and as a drug dealer," says Graham. "My character in this is just a *guy*, he's just a nice guy who gets involved in this whole big activity of taking the geese south."

That nice guy's role in the story is essential. Barry Strickland helps Thomas build the flying machines, and he teaches Amy to fly before becoming part of the vital ground-support team.

"He is one of the people driving the pickup truck," explains Graham, "with radios to tell them where they need to land and whether or not they're going to hit a storm. While those two are up in the air with the geese doing the beautiful banking across the sunsets, we're driving on to make sure the landing sites are safe."

Graham, like most of the cast, found there was something amazing about working with the geese. Of the moment when he called them down and was rewarded by having the entire flock land within a few yards of him, Graham says, "I'll remember that for a really, really long time."

Jeremy Ratchford, who plays the fictional character Glen Seaford, is the nearest thing to a villain in the film because it is his character's job to see that domestically raised wild geese have their wings clipped.

The ruling actually exists because domestically raised geese might introduce disease into wild flocks, and Bill Lishman had to get special permission to release his flocks into the wild.

C'mon Geese

Finally, what of the geese themselves? Were they destined to be ruined for life by their brush with Hollywood? Not for a moment as Bill Lishman explains: "We are mixing up science and entertainment here to some degree, but the birds we are raising for Hollywood will be migrating south, too. We will take them on the route, so they are being added to the experiment, and this year we will probably take fifty or sixty birds south with several aircraft."

So when audiences watch this incredible movie, they will know that the geese they see on screen left show business behind to settle into the serious business of their lives—heading north each spring to raise a family, then teaching the migration route they first learned from Bill Lishman to their offspring. But, should a crew be filming beside an inviting pond along the Atlantic Flyway some fall, they just might find some Canada geese stopping by to see if there are any old friends among them.

Bill Lishman on Flying with Birds

Color blindness kept Bill Lishman out of the air force, so in order to experience what he had watched so effortlessly practiced by birds, he took to hang gliding. He was a pioneer in ultralight aircraft, and as he tells it, one beautiful fall morning he was flying at about five hundred feet when a flock of ducks rose from a farmer's field and literally surrounded the little plane.

"I put the throttle on and our climb rate and everything was the same, and here I was in this huge . . . river of ducks, and I flew along with them for a couple of miles, and it was just amazing." Lishman goes on: "It was such an experience that when I landed, you know, tears were in my eyes, and I had to try and replicate that."

It took Lishman several years before he found somebody (wildlife consultant Bill Carrick) who taught him about imprinting birds. Lishman started with a small flock of fifteen goslings in 1986, succeeding in getting the birds to follow him on a motorcycle. By 1993, Lishman and Joe Duff were flying south with their first migrating flock of geese and succeeded in leading them to Virginia using two identical aircraft. The following year they went about twice as far, into South Carolina.

Before making the annual journey, the geese have to be conditioned to distance flights. Duff says, "We can also help them. You can tell when they're getting tired; their mouths open and they splay their feet to cool their bodies. So you can kind of pick them up." He explains that the geese learn to surf on the leading edge of the aircraft wings. "You can actually carry the birds and then, all of a sudden, they're fine to fly again."

Flying with birds can be a very intimate experience. Lishman says to check a bird's identification, a half-inch high number on a leg band, it is necessary to fly within about three feet of it. Switching to a pusher-engine mount allowed the birds to come closer without being in danger of the propeller. Lishman and Duff not only had to redesign and modify existing ultralight machines, they also had to contend with the red tape of Canada's federal government to obtain the necessary permits. They now carry some eight pieces of paper in each aircraft to prove what they are doing is legal.

"I think the next dream is really to try and get . . . whooping cranes migrating," Lishman says, referring to a surviving flock of barely 140 birds that migrate up to 3,000 miles from northern Canada to the Gulf coast of Texas. "The idea is to get a secondary flock . . . and start them somewhere in a different location . . . so they would learn (a new) migration route."

The Credits

COLUMBIA PICTURES presents a Sandollar production of *Fly Away Home*, directed by Carroll Ballard. The film stars Jeff Daniels, Anna Paquin, and Dana Delany. Terry Kinney, Holter Graham, and Jeremy Ratchford also star. *Fly Away Home* is produced by John Veitch and Carol Baum. The screenplay is by Robert Rodat and Vince McKewin based on the autobiography by Bill Lishman. Sandy Gallin is the executive producer. The distinguished behind-the-scenes team includes director of photography Caleb Deschanel, A.S.C. Nicholas C. Smith, A.C.E., is the editor. Séamus Flannery is the production designer with Marie-Sylvie Deveau serving as costume designer. The music is by Mark Isham.

Screenwriter **ROBERT RODAT** wrote the story and teleplay for the HBO movie *The Comrades of Summer*. He also wrote the critically acclaimed children's adventure *Tall Tale*. Screenwriter **VINCE MCKEWIN** wrote the feature film *Veteran's Day* and the script *The Climb*, starring John Hurt.

The record of **BILL LISHMAN'S** work with Operation Migration has been published in his autobiography entitled *Father Goose: The Adventures of a Wildlife Hero*, with photographs by Joseph Duff. An environmentalist and animal lover, he is also a metal sculptor of international renown and an inventor who designed his own underground house. He lives with his family on a farm east of Toronto in Ontario, Canada.

PATRICIA HERMES, author of the novelization of the screenplay, is also author of many highly acclaimed novels for children and young adults. Among her awards are: American Library Association Best Book, School Library Journal Best Book, and many Children's Choice Awards. Her previous books have included *Mama Let's Dance, On Winter's Wind,* and *The Cousins Club* series, as well as novelizations of *My Girl* and *My Girl 2*. She lives in Connecticut.

BABE
THE FILM STORYBOOK

Based on the film *Babe*
Adapted by Ron Fontes and
Justine Korman
From a screenplay by George Miller and
Chris Noonan
Based on the novel *The Sheep-Pig* by
Dick King-Smith

Nothing could have prepared Farmer
Hogget for the shock of seeing the piglet
he won at the fair herding chickens in the
farmyard. But when Babe is put to the
test, he proves to be a very
special pig indeed.

THE DEMON HEADMASTER STRIKES AGAIN
Gillian Cross

The villainous genius is back at his desk!

He's back, and he's very, very dangerous.

Dinah's father is headhunted for a new job at the Biodiversity Research Centre – and who should be the Director, but the Demon Headmaster . . .

This time his lust for power sees him meddling with evolution itself. The consequences of his evil schemes will be deadly if the SPLAT gang doesn't act – and fast.

JAMES AND THE GIANT PEACH
Roald Dahl

Now an amazing film!

Something is about to happen, James told himself. Something peculiar is about to happen at any moment.

James has lived with his two beastly aunts ever since the day his parents were eaten up outside London Zoo by an angry escaped rhinoceros. Aunt Sponge and Aunt Spiker are really horrible people. They make poor James's life a misery.

Then something very peculiar happens – something magical that is to completely change James's wretched existence and take him on the most amazing and unbelievable journey!

A classic story perfectly illustrated by Quentin Blake.

ROALD DAHL'S
MATILDA ACTIVITY BOOK
Illustrated by Quentin Blake

Matilda is an extraordinary girl with a
brilliant mind but she's stuck with
gormless parents and a hateful
headmistress. She may be small but her
determination is huge and she discovers
she is capable of some amazing things –
the monstrous grown-ups in her life are in
for a few surprises.

You don't need to be a genius to enjoy this
fun-packed collection. A treasure trove of
wordsearches, mazes, spot the difference
and other puzzles, all based on the
fantastic film *Matilda* and Roald Dahl's
well-loved book.

ROALD DAHL'S MATILDA SECRET FILE
Illustrated by Quentin Blake

By the time Matilda starts school, she can do complicated mathematical sums in her head and has read most of the books in her public library. Her kind teacher, Miss Honey, is convinced she is a genius while her parents and headmistress make her life a misery. Matilda soon discovers that being a genius has its advantages and she has a few tricks up her sleeve for those monstrous grown-ups . . .

If you think you can match Matilda in the brains department, you'll love this puzzle extravaganza! A brain-busting collection of quizzes, mathematical conundrums and many other tricky challenges based on Roald Dahl's best-selling book and the *Matilda* film.

MATT'S MILLION
Andrew Norriss

Now a brilliant TV series

Dear Matthew, I have great pleasure in enclosing a cheque, made out to your name, for the sum of £1,227,309.87.

Matt Collins is eleven years old, and a millionaire! Suddenly he has the money to buy anything he wants – a mansion or even a Rolls-Royce. But being rich is more difficult than he thought.

THE ADVENTURES OF PINOCCHIO™
Carlo Collodi
A novelization by J. J. Gardner
Based on the screenplay by Sherry Mills
and Steve Barron and Tom Benedek and
Barry Berman

"You're a puppet, Pinocchio – you're not a real boy."

Pinocchio is a special puppet. He can walk and talk, and his nose grows when he tells a lie! However, more than anything in the world, he wants to be a real boy.

Before Pinocchio's wish can come true he must prove he has a heart. He has to learn to tell the truth and care enough to cry real tears. But, with the help of a talking cricket, Pinocchio learns that miracles can happen.

THE QUEEN'S NOSE: HARMONY'S RETURN

Steve Attridge
Adapted from the BBC TV series

Wishes can come true . . .

. . . especially if you are Harmony Parker
with a lucky 50p piece. What other people
don't understand, however, is exactly how
powerful that curious coin is. In the wrong
hands, matters can get out of hand. Mr
Slingit, the headmaster, discovers this
when he wishes all his pupils would
vanish, and school bully Stub Martin finds
his perfect prank turns into a foaming
nightmare.

As for Harmony, she's got her gruesome
gran, her spiteful sister and her bankrupt
dad to contend with. Never in the history
of mankind has a 50p piece had
to work so hard.

WIND IN THE WILLOWS
NOVELISATION
Adapted by Nancy Krulik
From the screenplay by Terry Jones
Based on the novel by Kenneth Grahame

The fastest Toad on the road.

Life along the river bank is quiet and relaxing. That is, until poor Mole has his home destroyed and Toad discovers motor cars.

What follows is a thrilling adventure, as Ratty, Mole and Badger try to save Toad from himself and Toad Hall from destruction.

Based on the classic story by Kenneth Grahame and the film starring Terry Jones.

READ MORE IN PUFFIN

For children of all ages, Puffin represents quality and variety – the very best in publishing today around the world.

For complete information about books available from Puffin – and Penguin – and how to order them, contact us at the appropriate address below. Please note that for copyright reasons the selection of books varies from country to country.

On the worldwide web: www.puffin.co.uk

In the United Kingdom: Please write to *Dept. EP, Penguin Books Ltd, Bath Road, Harmondsworth, West Drayton, Middlesex UB7 ODA*

In the United States: Please write to *Consumer Sales, Penguin USA, P.O. Box 999, Dept. 17109, Bergenfield, New Jersey 07621-0120*. VISA and MasterCard holders call 1-800-253-6476 to order Penguin titles

In Canada: Please write to *Penguin Books Canada Ltd, 10 Alcorn Avenue, Suite 300, Toronto, Ontario M4V 3B2*

In Australia: Please write to *Penguin Books Australia Ltd, P.O. Box 257, Ringwood, Victoria 3134*

In New Zealand: Please write to *Penguin Books (NZ) Ltd, Private Bag 102902, North Shore Mail Centre, Auckland 10*

In India: Please write to *Penguin Books India Pvt Ltd, 706 Eros Apartments, 56 Nehru Place, New Delhi 110 019*

In the Netherlands: Please write to *Penguin Books Netherlands bv, Postbus 3507, NL-1001 AH Amsterdam*

In Germany: Please write to *Penguin Books Deutschland GmbH, Metzlerstrasse 26, 60594 Frankfurt am Main*

In Spain: Please write to *Penguin Books S. A., Bravo Murillo 19, 1° B, 28015 Madrid*

In Italy: Please write to *Penguin Italia s.r.l., Via Felice Casati 20, I–20124 Milano*

In France: Please write to *Penguin France S. A., 17 rue Lejeune, F–31000 Toulouse*

In Japan: Please write to *Penguin Books Japan, Ishikiribashi Building, 2–5–4, Suido, Bunkyo-ku, Tokyo 112*

In South Africa: Please write to *Longman Penguin Southern Africa (Pty) Ltd, Private Bag X08, Bertsham 2013*